Loathing

Temptation

Loathing Temptation

By Caz May

First Published 2021
Paperback ISBN 978-0-6488534-6-6

Published by Caz May

© Caz May 2020
Cover image from iStock
Cover editing by Caz May

To my fellow insomniacs.
And all the crazy thoughts that fill our brains at 1am.

Author's Preface

Hey lovely readers!
From the moment Ashton popped into my head I felt
consumed by his story.
Both of the tropes in this story are some of my
absolute favourites to read and I'm so glad I can
share one of my own stories of these tropes, with
you, my readers.

I hope you enjoy Ashton & Tempany's story.
Please take note of the trigger warning.

Caz May
xx

Trigger Warning

Please be aware there are some dark themes in this story, from the start in the prologue and throughout the story.

Some parts may be confronting and triggering to readers sensitive to child abuse and sexual abuse.
And also there is mention of drug and alcohol addiction, and suicide.

This story is set in Australia, where the age of consent is sixteen. Please do not comment on this in regard to the story in reviews and such.

Playlist

Below is the playlist of songs for this story. They're in no particular order. The Spotify playlist QR code is at the bottom.

1. Crush-Cigarettes After Sex
2. Oxygen-Winona Oak
3. What have you done-Within Temptation
4. He don't love me-Winona Oak
5. Unconditional-Picture This
6. Sinning with you-Sam Hunt
7. Falling in love-Cigarettes after sex
8. My thoughts on you-The Band CAMINO
9. Naked-Jake Scott
10. Breaking Me-Topic/A7S
11. Worthy of you- Plested
12. Chew on my heart-James Bay
13. Nobody Else-Cole Norton
14. Fight for Love-Blue October feat Blue Reed
15. Bad Things-Jace Everett
16. Oh my my-Blue October
17. Cherry Twist-Becoming Young
18. Wild Love (Acoustic)-James Bay
19. Karma, Come Back-Incubus
20. Run-Matt Nathanson
21. Kill me slow-David Guetta, MORTEN
22. Falling (Acoustic Mashup)- Landon Austin
23. Shiver - Coldplay

Also by Caz May

My Girl Duet

Bk 1-Not my Girl
Bk 2-Still my Girl

Always Only You Series

Bk 1-Roommates Don't Kiss & Tell
Bk 2-Friends Don't Say Goodbye
Bk 3-Feelings Don't Play Fair
Bk 4-Hearts Don't Steer Us Wrong

The Mackenney Family Saga

Bk 1-Country Secrets
Bk 2-Doctor Attraction
Bk 3-Unlawful Attachment

A Holiday Romance Duet

Bk 1-Take Flight

The only way to get rid of a temptation is to yield to it.

Oscar Wilde

Prologue

Ashton

Dribbling my basketball I shoot for the hoop. Again—for the umpteenth time—I miss. Muttering a curse word under my breath I can hear my father's berating words in my head, *'you're useless boy'*. I hate that his words get to me, hate that they tear at my insides.

I'm useless at playing basketball, but it's all I want to do. Not being able to get into the Under ten's for another year, I'm spending every waking minute practising. But it's not like I'll be able to play even if I get in. Daddy dearest won't have it. Even now, he's trying to make me like numbers so I can be a big shot

Loathing Temptation

businessman like him, but I don't understand stuff like Maths. School sucks—except when I'm playing basketball at recess with Zeke—my best friend from kindergarten, Ezekiel Alessio. He's like a brother to me, and sometimes I wish he was because other than my kid sister Ava and my mum I'd much rather have a different family. Zeke's dad is the polar opposite of mine, supportive and loving.

My dad wouldn't know what love meant if someone beat him over the head with it. He says the words to me sometimes, but then his actions show me hatred. Fidel Castello breathes hatred.

It seeps out of his skin.

I'm still bouncing my ball, loving the sound of the rubber hitting the concrete and the feeling playing basketball gives me. Stepping side to side, I bounce the ball between my legs, psyching myself up to make the shot, and sink it through the hoop this time. And that's when I see her, standing next to the court in a little tutu dress. She's smiling, just like the last time she came to the park and watched me play.

She ran up to me then, taking the basketball and bouncing it; whilst giggling. I meekly introduced myself and she told me her name was Tempany Davies. I'd thought it was a weird name, but it kinda suits her.

Every time I come to the park basketball court I wonder if she's going to turn up, and give me her sweet smiles that make my tummy feel funny.

I can't help but smile now when she runs up to play with me, expertly snatching the ball away from me, starting to bounce it whilst I'm struck stupid by her. I'm sure she's the same age as me, but she seems younger.

She crouches down, about to shoot for the hoop, and most likely sink it when a voice starts calling her name from across the park.

"Tempany, Tempany, it's time to go, baby." She smiles shyly, and runs across the court, away from me.

It's then—looking down at my empty hands—that I realise she took my ball. She ran off clutching my basketball against her tummy.

And I know that this time I'm going to be in big trouble. My dad's warning about what he was going to do to me if I came home without my ball again are in my head, and walking across the park to go home hot tears are stinging my eyes, thinking about the pain I'm about to endure.

Pushing the front door open, I tiptoe inside, hoping to sneak upstairs without my dad seeing me. But of course no such luck. I hear his voice—from the formal lounge—before I see him.

"Ashton, get in here boy," he shouts at me.

He's clenching his fists, crunching a piece of paper in between his fingers. "You want to tell me how the fuck you get an F in Mathematics?"

The hot tears are stinging my eyes again. And I mumble, "I don't get it, Dad."

"You don't get it! You don't get it, because you don't damn well apply yourself, boy. Always at that fucking basketball court."

Loathing Temptation

"I...I...I'm..."

"Spit it out boy!"

"I'm sorry, Daddy. I'll do better. I'll try harder, I promise."

"That's not good enough, Ashton. You shouldn't have to do better."

He stands up from the couch, stalking towards me. I'm trembling, knowing what's coming next, and knowing that this time is going to be worse than the times before.

His dark blue eyes look down to my empty hands, and even deeper anger flashes in them, making them seem black—like his heart—when he realises I'm not clutching a basketball.

"Where is your basketball, Ashton?"

I bite my lip, mumbling through my teeth. "A...a...girl...stole it."

He scoffs. "You expect me to believe that rot, Ashton. You know what happens when you lie to me, boy."

His words make my tummy feel sick. I know what happens when I tell fibs, but I'd rather get hit than have him hit Ava or Mummy.

"I'm telling the truth. Someone took it."

He's fuming at me, like a bull out in the paddocks down the road. His words are loud when he responds, "That's the fifth basketball you've 'lost' Ashton. Shit like that doesn't grow on trees. You need to learn your lesson about the value of property."

"I don't get you, Daddy," I reply meekly, fighting back tears.

He doesn't reply then, and I step back, desperately wanting to escape the room when his hands start to undo his belt. I hear the sound of the leather cracking when he yanks it out of the loops on his pants.

And I gulp, telling my feet to move, to run from him. But I can't. I can't move an inch, or the beating will be worse. I don't like that daddy does this to me.

"Pants down boy," daddy commands, wrapping the end of his belt around his fist.

My knees are wobbly as I slip my trackies down to my ankles. The cold air hits my bum, and I brace myself for the first hit. Again I hear the crack of the leather and then the smack of it against my skin. It burns, and I bite the inside of my cheek to stop the scream escaping my mouth.

Daddy moves closer to me, caging me in. And without giving me any warning, his belt cracks against my bum again.

One. Two. Three. Four.

I'm counting in my head, wondering how many times he's going to smack the leather against my backside. It's practically numb but is also throbbing and I just want it to be over so I can run to my bed and cry myself to sleep.

I close my eyes then, waiting for the final blow of the belt against my skin, but it doesn't come and I feel relief rush through me for a moment, until the heel of Daddy's hand smacks harder against my skin.

Once. Twice.

Six smacks. Six markings on my skin. And this time they hurt so much more than they ever have.

I hate my daddy.

But now I also hate Tempany Davies.

She did this to me because she took my basketball.

Loathing Temptation

One

Ashton

---

10 years later

It feels surreal that this day is finally here. The first day of year twelve, the last year before I can get the fuck out of Lockgrove Bay, and move to the city where my dad can't find me.

Unless mum opens her trap.

She might be free of him according to the divorce papers but he still controls her every move, holding money over her and using the house as collateral; a bargaining chip so Mum jumps when he says so.

I'd cut him off to—the prick—but he pays my way, pays my school fees for Lockgrove Preparatory. And that means I can own the hallways as captain of the elite Lockgrove Lions for this final year in hell.

Turning the Camaro into my reserved car park, I cut the engine, grabbing my gym bag and slinging it over my shoulder. Glancing around the courtyard, I sigh looking at all the familiar faces, and feeling a knot twist in my stomach. Every damn person looks like they took some happy pills—some molly—over the summer holidays and they're all floating into Lockgrove Preparatory like they actually want to be here.

I'd rather be as far away as possible. Especially because Mum has told me my new stepsister is likely to be starting school today, and when I meet her I'm expected to play nice.

She's only told me her name is Te and she's in year eleven.

Like I should actually even give a fuck.

I have a sister, I don't need another one. Ava's a brat—a sweet one—but still a brat and making sure she doesn't get herself into trouble at school is enough shit to deal with, with basketball, and trying not to flunk Maths so daddy dearest lays off. I don't need anymore girl drama.

Tentatively I walk across the courtyard, and I'm startled by a slap on the back.

"Hey dipshit, you got ya balls back yet?"

I laugh, slapping my hand against my best mate Zeke's in greeting.

"Hey bro. And yeah I put my big boy daks on. Fallon can go fuck a tree."

Loathing Temptation

"Wouldn't put it past her. She'd fuck anything."

"Harsh, mate."

"You aside, man. Still don't know why you tapped that when you could have had your pick, and played the court."

We walk in the front gate, and I spot my ex-girlfriend Fallon Warner sauntering towards me with a fake smile. She's done up to the nines, like she's going out clubbing—not to school—her face caked in makeup that's the wrong shade for her skin tone.

And she quite frankly looks like a clown who's been dragged through the bush backwards and then drowned in the ocean.

Her heavily made up cheeks are streaked with mascara from tears. And I couldn't give a flying fuck.

She stops me from continuing to walk inside with Zeke, grabbing my arm.

"Hi Ash,"she bleats at me, all sweet but her voice is grating on me.

Whatever the fuck I saw in her, I have no idea. Probably the fact she can suck a dick like a damn vacuum.

"Ash, I'm sorry baby," she says again, looking at me with tears starting to drip down her cheeks again.

"Whatever, Fallon. You're a skank, and a shit root. Go fuck a tree."

"Ash, why? Why are you being like this?"

"Like what? A guy who had enough of your clingy bullshit?"

"I...I...I'm not clingy. I love you, Ashton."

I laugh at her, starting to walk away and again she grabs my arm, clinging onto me like a damn monkey. She hadn't exactly done anything wrong, unless you count scaring the ever loving shit out of me by telling me she was pregnant over the summer holidays.

It was in fact a lie, and I dumped her arse the second I found out she was trying to trap me.

I fucking loathe liars. Daddy dearest spits lies out, every second word out of his mouth. And I hate admitting to myself that I've told my own fair share of lies—to protect my mum and sister from Fidel Castello—that my own self loathing runs deep. He also constantly feeds me the *'you're useless Ashton, you're not worthy of the Castello name.'*

I want to make him proud, but I probably never will. Nothing I do, nothing I want to do, my Basketball first and foremost is good enough for him. And it's the one thing I'm actually good at.

Fallon breaks my thoughts with her whining voice, "Ashton, please. Please just give me another chance."

Her begging is so fucking pathetic.

"Seriously, Fallon. Fuck off. We are done."

I snatch my arm back and head inside, just as the morning bell sounds. And stepping through the double doors heading to my locker, my eyes lock on an ash blonde girl walking down the hallway towards me.

My stomach twists. And bile rises into my throat.

It's been ten years, but I'd know her anywhere.

And fuck.

I'm fucking dreaming.

I have to be fucking dreaming right?

She isn't here.

She doesn't even live in Lockgrove Bay anymore.

Loathing Temptation

But my eyes are not deceiving me, because even when I rub them to stop myself from hallucinating, she's still here. And she's opening a locker, stretching up on her tiptoes.

Her short tutu dress rides up, practically giving me a view of her breakfast and a hot curvy arse that's covered by shiny white tights.

Fuck. She's gorgeous. A temptress.

But. No. Fucking. Way. I hate her.

I hate Tempany Davies.

And now she's here I'm going to make her life hell, just like mine has been for the last ten years, because of her.

Two

Tempany

*H*oisting my backpack onto my shoulder I take slow steps into Lockgrove Bay preparatory.

My stomach is in knots and I'm regretting my outfit choice of a pink tutu long-sleeved skater dress with white opaque tights.

I don't know why I yanked it out of my wardrobe this morning —maybe nostalgia—but it's short, and heading down the hallway I'm stretching the jersey fabric down so it at least reaches my knees and not halfway up my thighs.

This outfit is the old Tempany, not the new me.

Not, Te.

Loathing Temptation

And coming back to Lockgrove Bay after ten years I want to blend into the background, not stand out. Blending in will hopefully ensure that he—Ashton Castello—doesn't notice me.

Leaving him behind when I was seven broke my heart. He gave me butterflies in my belly, and his smile made me want to giggle. Not a day has passed where I haven't thought of him, but Facebook searching over the years has made my feelings for him more intense. He's beyond gorgeous, and so far out of my league, I'd have more chance of snagging a boyfriend from my fave romance novel than having Ashton notice me. He's most likely forgotten about the shy little girl who learnt how to play basketball so she could play with him.

Turning the corner, I'm in front of a row of lockers, and glance at the piece of paper I'm clutching in my sweaty palm. *Locker 1220.*

I yank it open, haphazardly pushing my backpack in the bottom, and unzipping it to grab out my rainbow unicorn pencil case. I should have gotten a new one—as I'm sure to be teased—but I love the worn look of it and it's done me well for the last five years. I know I partly keep it because it was the last thing Mum gave me before she died.

Five years have passed and I still can't get the image of her limp body out of my mind. I can still see the whole scene of when I found her dead in the bathroom of our tiny flat, bottles of pills strewn across the floor and the stench of vomit in the air.

I swallow the lump and bile in my throat down, grabbing out the rest of my books for first period; English.

I can do this. New Tempany—well Te—can do this.

One foot in front of the other, Te.

Turning to head back down the hallway, I swear when the bell sounds I can feel eyes on me. Eyes that can see through my stupid outfit. And eyes that know the old me.

But when I turn around the hallways are filling with students—at lockers—hugging and kissing and no one is giving me a second glance.

If I keep to myself, go to the library during break times and straight home to Dad's after school I won't see him.

But I kinda want to see him in person to see if he remembers me.

And maybe—in my dreams—he might just want the new me.

Loathing Temptation

Three

Ashton

E ven after Tempany heads back down the corridor and the halls start to fill with my classmates, I'm still standing by my locker, in a goddamn daze.

She looked fucking sinful in that outfit. And I hate that Ash Jnr had decided to throb in my daks. Thank fuck for black basketball shorts, as they can hide a boner better than grey ones.

I gulp, grabbing the rest of my books out for the hell of first period, first day back at school and in my case every Monday morning hell, as I have Maths.

I'm still stupid when it comes to Maths, I'll never understand numbers and formulas like Dad.

He's deluded, thinking I'll be a businessman like him. I just want to play basketball and being Captain I'm hoping a scholarship to play at uni is on the cards. Anything to get out of Lockgrove Bay.

Slamming my locker shut, I turn to head down the hallway and find Zeke standing next to me, grinning.

"You right mate?"

"Yeah, why?"

"You look like you've seen a ghost or some shit."

"You could say that," I reply, biting down on my lip, trying to not let images of Tempany in that outfit fill my head.

Zeke follows me down the corridor.

"What gives man? You're acting like a nutter today. I don't think Fallon gave you your balls back."

I push the door of the classroom open, actually early for the final bell, and give my best mate dagger eyes when we sit down next to each other.

"She's back, Zeke."

"Who?"

"You know who."

"Melody?" he asks, referring to the chick who got knocked up by our teammate Grant. I wanna slap him about the head for being so daft.

"No, you dipshit. Her."

He glares at me, recognition hitting his mind.

"Her? Her? As in Tempany?"

"Yes, her," I snap at him before laughing when Mr Daniels clears his throat from the front of the room. He looks like a wanker, with a dick up his gay arse.

Loathing Temptation

He presses his palms into the desk, sticking his arse in the air, and I chuckle under my breath, elbowing Zeke.

"Mr D looks like he's taking the 'd' up his tight arse," I whisper to my best mate. He cracks up, and Mr Daniels seethes.

From up the front, Mr Daniels then glares at my best mate with steam practically coming out of his ears.

"Would you care to share what's so funny, Ezekiel?" Mr Daniels demands, balling his fists and giving Zeke dagger eyes. He most certainly has a dick up his arse or needs one if he's not getting any.

Zeke sniggers, his eyes darting to me for a moment. "Well, Mr D, Ashton just said he was wondering if you played with any balls over the summer?"

Mr D almost screams out some angry slur. But curbs his sudden anger by clenching his fists tighter. The whole class erupts into laughter and Mr D goes tomato red, which obviously means he did play with some balls over the summer holidays.

Stupid gay tosser.

"Ezekiel that is highly inappropriate and my personal life is none of your business."

Zeke laughs again, making Mr D even angrier. I can't help but laugh too. Seeing Mr D getting riled up is fucking hilarious.

"Ezekiel, Ashton, detention now! Get out of my classroom, now!" Mr D roars at us both, making the room fall silent, except for the collective gasp of our classmates' shock at Mr D actually taking charge for once.

Zeke and I gather up our books and leave the room, breaking into a fit of laughter the moment we step out the door. Zeke gives an up yours to Mr D through the glass of the door, and Mr D opens

Caz May

it suddenly, shoving a piece of paper into my hand to take to detention.Heading down the corridor to the detention hall at the end, I slap Zeke on the back.

"Thanks for that man. I fucking hate Maths and Mr Dick lover."

"No worries man. And I happen to know that Miss Miller is on duty in detention."

"Damn, sweet as."

"Yep," he replies, opening the door to the detention room, and smiling at Miss Miller. He tried to get it on with her last year, but she shot him down of course. But she's always been easy on us and all the guys from the team.

She laughs when we both walk in, and asks, "What are you idiots doing here first day back? And first period?"

I laugh, handing her the detention slip when Zeke answers, "I asked Mr D if he played with any balls over the holidays."

She cracks up laughing. "Zeke, you didn't?"

"Guilty Miss M. You should've seen his face. Gold. Well, tomato red actually."

"Well, I don't have to tell you that's not appropriate but it's definitely funny, I'll give you that."

"And I had to get my boy here out of Maths class."

"Right, well first day back and all I'm guessing you don't have any homework, so chill. I'll tell Mr Daniels I made you do Algebra equations."

"Thanks, Miss M," Zeke says cheekily, giving her a wink that colours her cheeks.

We sit down, and I elbow him.

"You still wanna root her, don't you?"

"Yeah, I've got eyes, Ash. Miss M is hot."

Loathing Temptation

"You're a wanker."

"Guilty," he replies laughing. "So tell me more about Tempany? Is she hot?"

I gulp, thinking about Tempany earlier this morning, imagining her wearing no tights under that tutu.

"Ash, man, I said is she hot or what?

"Yeah man, she's fucking gorgeous but I can't."

He stares at me, shock on his face. He knows about Tempany taking my basketball.

"So, you're not going to root a gorgeous chick because she took your ball when you were eight?"

Anger rises in my chest. And I ball my fists, wanting to punch my best mate for being such a hard arsed, sex-driven wanker. I'm so pissed at him for acting like he doesn't give a fucking shit about what Tempany taking my basketball did to me.

"It's not that so much man...it's that because of that dad beat my arse so hard."

Zeke is dumbfounded. I'd never told him that little—well not so little—detail about Dad laying into me because of the basketball incident, only that Tempany took it.

"Shit, man I didn't know. Your dad is such a fucking prick."

"Prick isn't a harsh enough word for him. You know that bro. And what he did to me because of Tempany I'll never forget. He's been on my arse ever since, beating the shit out of me for any little thing. I hate her so fucking much. She ruined my fucking life."

Zeke frowns, touching my arm. "Yeah I get ya, bro, so ruin hers."

I chuckle, almost manically. "I plan to. I'm going love fucking her up."

"Oh yeah, you think she's pure?"

"I'd guarantee it, and I'm going to bring the temptress to her knees."

He laughs maniacally. "Yeah, man. Fuck yeah."

"I love ya, man."

"Don't get all sappy on me dipshit. I don't bat for that team."

"Haha, go fuck yourself."

He pushes his chair back. And grabs his dick through his trackies, making a wanking gesture with his fist. And I cack myself laughing when he starts moaning and leaning back in his chair.

"Zeke!" Miss Miller's voice calls out from the front of the room.

He stops his fake dick wanking, looking right at her and fluttering his eyelashes. "Yes, Miss M? You wanna join me?"

"No Zeke."

"Shame, Miss M. You'd love it."

"That's enough, Ezekiel!"

He laughs at her, and I can't help but laugh at my best mate. He's such a tease.

"Burn, Miss M. Burn."

She doesn't get to reply, the bell cajoling through the speakers.

"Well, Miss M, it's been fun, but we're out. Catch ya in *'physical'* education," Zeke taunts, drawling out the word physical and rocking his hips in a sexual gesture. Walking out we hear her laughter.

I turn to head in the opposite direction to Zeke, calling out, "Catch ya at recess, dipshit. Keep ya dick in your pants until then."

"Maybe, and catch ya then," he calls back to me.

Loathing Temptation

I head down the hallway to English class, thinking about ways to fuck with Tempany.

The little temptress isn't going to know whats hit her.

I'm going to ruin her, and enjoy every second.

Four

Tempany

*T*he moment the recess bell rings through the classroom, every single one of my classmates jumps out of their seats, rushing out of the classroom. I hang back a moment, waiting for the classroom to clear and for the craziness to die down in the hallways. I've been on edge ever since I got to school, since we drove into Lockgrove Bay again; a week ago.

I'd been itching to go to the beach, but I'd kept to myself, even when my best friend Lorena was face timing me, eager to don new bikini's and go to tease the boys. She's the only person I kept in contact with since I left, but we never talked about what was happening in Lockgrove Bay. It hurt to much that everyone had grown up with the call of the waves, and the sea air, whilst I'd had to endure red dirt and the smell of poo up my nose every day, stuck in the country in a rotting house with Mum's poor excuse for a human boyfriend.

Sometimes, in my dreams, I can still feel his grimy hands on me, his dry lips on mine, and I wake up in a cold sweat fighting with my sheets in a panic.

At least being back in Lockgrove Bay, I can soak up the sun, and try to find some peace again.

Dad's new job at the local architecture firm was due to start soon, and I was happy for him, to be able to finally do what he'd always wanted.

The resentment still bubbled inside me though, resentment that he didn't take me with him when he left Mum.

But I try to block those thoughts out most of the time, including now as I head out of the now empty classroom to my locker. The hallways are practically empty and shoving my books inside my locker I grab out a muesli bar and my phone.

I type Lorena a text.

where am I meeting you?

Her reply is instant.

bleachers by the b—ball court

um ok

I tuck my phone into the sleeve of my cardigan and head outside. The whole courtyard is abuzz with students catching up about the holidays and it makes me feel uneasy. I'm nervous about seeing Lorena again. I'm surprised she still wants to be my friend after coming to visit me in hell just before mum died. But when I'd told her I was coming back to Lockgrove Bay for good she squealed in delight and has been in my ear about everything I've been missing out on, and everything we have to do this year.

Reaching the basketball courts, I glance around at the students playing a game. Of course, my eyes are drawn to him.

Ashton.

And he looks gorgeous, in basketball shorts that are low on his hips, showing off the v of his muscles. He's shirtless and his abs are defined and glistening with sweat. He's clearly in his element and much better at playing basketball than he was when we were kids.

Old me would have gone up to him and joined in, stolen the ball and shot for goal. But the new me is to shy and dying just looking at him.

My mouth is watering, and I gulp down the excessive amount of saliva in my mouth when I hear Lorena's voice calling out my name, "Tem, over here!"

I spot her sitting at the top of the bleachers and telling my feet to move I head up them to join her.

"Hey Lo," I greet her, pulling her into a tight hug.

Pulling back she smiles at me. "I can't believe you're actually here. We have so much to catch up on."

Loathing Temptation

"Yeah," I reply sheepishly, not meeting her eyes on mine, but again staring down at Ashton.

Lorena's voice breaks the silence. "They're gods huh?"

"What? Who?" I stammer, taking a big bite of my muesli bar and chewing loudly.

"Ashton and Zeke, dufus. You can't stop staring at them."

"Um yeah. I...um..."

She laughs, playfully poking me. "Tell me Tem. Ash or Zeke?"

I gulp, nearly choking on my bite of muesli bar. "Ashton. But he'd never go for me."

"He might. He just broke up with his girlfriend."

My eyes boggle, but I shake my head. "Still, I'm not his type."

"You never know Tem," she tells me smiling.

"Yeah, and please Lo, can you call me Te. I want to start new. It's hard enough coming back without people thinking about the old me."

"No worries, Te," she replies smiling. "So I hear there's a party at some year twelve guys house on Friday."

"And? Wouldn't we need to be invited?"

"No, dufus. So many people go to these things. We just show up, and get Ashton to notice you by you wearing something sexy."

"I don't think so, Lorena. I just want to lay low. You know, Friday night in."

"Oh Te, come on. It'll be fun, and we can crash at yours after."

"Lo, I don't know. I don't think Dad would be happy about me going to a party."

"Then we won't tell him."

"Yeah, I guess. He does have a date with his new lady friend on Friday night."

"Then it's sorted. I'll come over after school, and once your Dad leaves we'll get ready."

"Um, ok I guess. I'll just have to make sure it's ok for you to sleep over."

"Great, I'm so excited. It will be just like old times. I've missed you so much Te."

"I've missed you to," I reply standing up when the bell goes.

We walk past the students still milling around on the basketball court, and this time my staring makes Ashton catch my eye as he slips his white t-shirt back on.

I lick my lips, and he glares at me, anger flaring in his grey-blue eyes that makes my stomach hurt.

I don't know what I did to deserve that look, but it both scares and excites me.

I think the best idea—despite what Lorena thinks—is to steer clear of Ashton Castello, even though I feel like I'm drawn to him, like a moth to a flame.

Five

Ashton

*P*hysical education is my last class for a Monday, and most of the time it's boring as hell because Miss Miller insists we play and do any sport other than basketball.

The only good thing about the class is watching all the girls strut around in their netball skirts.

Last year my eyes would have been on Fallon, watching her doing high kicks, and practically showing the entire class her pussy. I'd loved that the dirty bitch always wore g-strings under her netball skirt, even though they're the shortest skirts around.

But now my eyes are drawn to my temptress.

Caz May

Miss Miller has us all lined up on the basketball court and hands us skipping ropes. Us boys are lined up on one side and the girls on the other.

I can't help but stare across at Tem in a netball skirt. I lick my lips suggestively, my eyes on hers. She drops her gaze to the ground, blushing.

It turns me on when I can make a chick blush.

Zeke looks over at me. And I can see his smirk out of the corner of my eyes.

"You gonna crack a fat, man?" He jeers at me loudly.

"Nah why you ratting me?"

"You're fucking someone with that stare right now, bro."

I turn to glare at my best mate, tempted to whack him in the head with my skipping rope.

"Fuck off. But fuck she looks ripper in that damn skirt."

His eyes gaze across at the girls, and he chuckles. "Well, netty skirts were invented to be torture. And also be easy to remove when said torture is too much to handle for horny wankers like yourself."

"Talk about yourself much," I taunt my best mate.

He's about to reply when he gulps down his words with Miss Miller standing in front of us.

"Do you boys not know how to skip or are you choosing not to?"

He licks his lips, his eyes grazing over Miss M's body, straight to her netball skirt.

"Ezekiel, my eyes are up here," she bellows at him, nodding her head upwards. "And you will answer me or you'll be in detention again, with Mr Daniels."

Loathing Temptation

Damn, Zeke just got owned.

He gulps again, looking at me. I'm trying not to laugh, but watching my best mate go down in flames is beyond hilarious.

"I don't know how to skip Miss M. Scouts honour."

"Sure you don't, Ezekiel. Drop the rope and do ten laps of the oval instead."

I can't help but let out the laugh I've been holding in. "And you Ashton can join him, but double the laps."

"Aww come on Miss M. That's not fair," I protest, giving her puppy dog eyes.

"I'm not going easy on you dufuses this year. Grow some balls."

I really have to stifle my laugh this time, for sure to land my arse in detention again if I say anything else.

Sauntering past the girls who are being all prissy and skipping, I lift my t-shirt over my head and throw it at Tempany's head.

She shrieks grabbing it in a fist, and I'll be damned—she fucking sniffs it. Not fucking kidding, she inhales it like a hit of crack. And scrunches it into a fist, throwing it back at me.

Everyone's eyes are glaring at us both. And I call out to her, "You keep it Tem!" whilst throwing the t-shirt back at her again. She huffs angrily, making everyone laugh.

Fuck it's fun taunting her.

After doing my twenty laps, I'm wrecked, but Miss Miller has decided that we need to be tortured more and has us all competing—boys vs girls—for football.

Tem is a bumbling idiot, every time she gets the ball, she falls all over the place. But it's because she can't stop staring at me. And I have to admit I'm digging it.

I still hate her, but seeing her obvious lust for me makes taunting her much more fun. She trips over a lump of grass, falling at my feet. And I laugh hard, standing over her as she tries to stand up.

"Good to see you on your knees Tem. Next time play nice with my balls whilst you're down there."

She huffs at me again, standing up and rushing away with tears in her eyes. She throws the ball back at me, and I catch it, calling out, "You can throw, Tem. But can you suck?"

She turns back to glare at me, about to charge at me when the bell rings and Miss Miller is yelling at us to head to the change rooms.

She stops me a moment.

"You need to watch your language and attitude around Tempany. She's not had it easy these last few years Ashton."

I give Miss Miller a sweet—fake—smile. "Noted Miss M. I'm sorry."

I'm not sorry. Tempany ruined my life, and I've only just started ruining hers.

The end of day bell has rung, and Tempany still hasn't ventured out of the girls change room.

Zeke gives me a high five, leaning against the wall by the girls change rooms, whilst I head inside.

Loathing Temptation

Quickly darting between the lockers, I check to see if everyone has cleared out, which they have, except for Tempany. She's still in her netball skirt but has her t-shirt off. The sight of her in just a bra and her netball skirt is fucking hot.

I head in further, stepping up behind her.

"Damn temptress, you waiting for me?" I tease, caging her against the lockers with my body pressed against hers. Her breath hitches, but she doesn't reply. I lean closer to her, whispering in her ear, "You're going to fall to your knees for me again, Temptress, and you're going to love every damn second of it."

She lets out a moan, and rocking my semi-hard cock—that's risen enough to lift up the hem of her skirt—against her arse I moan into her ear. And without warning, I grip her waist and turn her around to face me. She whimpers, staring at me with hooded eyes.

Her grey irises give away her lust for me. Leaning in, my face is just a centimetre away from hers, and her heart is clearly pounding in her chest.

I don't doubt her pussy is wet as fuck for me, but I'm not going to give her the satisfaction of feeling my touch where she wants it most; not yet.

I press my forehead to hers, my lips brushing so close to hers, almost kissing her and I whisper, "I loathe you, Tempany."

She shoves her hands against my chest, grunting and huffing again. I laugh, grabbing the waistband of her skirt and ripping it off of her.

She makes some odd wailing sound, whimpering and sobbing when I walk out, holding up her skirt in my hand.

Zeke is still waiting outside and he smirks at me, eyeing the skirt in my hand. "You got a trophy for taking her, huh?"

"Nah, just riled her up. And thought I'd take her skirt as a reminder of the *I want you Ashton'* look on her face."

"You're an arse man," he jeers at me, slapping me on the back as we head towards our lockers down the corridor. "Love ya hard."

"Guilty and rack off," I jeer back, glancing down the hallway to see if Tempany has ventured out of the change rooms yet.

She looked fucking sexy in her lacy knickers and bra.

I shake the dirty thoughts away because I shouldn't be thinking about Tempany that way.

I hate her.

And also because Zeke is waving his arms in my face.

"Hey, fucktard...I said aren't you down for playing duty today?"

"Nah, always man, mine in twenty.

"Yeah bro, out," he replies, giving me our signature hand slap and hip bump greeting.

He heads out to his shitbox of a car—that I'm surprised even made it to school—and I follow after walking back past the change rooms.

I can hear Tempany sobbing, and I should feel upset. But it makes me feel giddy that I'm getting to her. And I'm only just getting started.

Loathing Temptation

Six

Ashton

Sitting on the chaise in the rumpus room, I'm about to throw my controller across the room. Zeke is whipping my arse at Call of Duty, and he's hollering out, "Fuck yeah!" at the top of his lungs.

He shoots my character dead, and I throw my controller on the floor in frustration.

I can't even concentrate on playing video games, without thinking about the look in Tempany's eyes when I nearly kissed her.

Fuck. I nearly kissed her. Fucking kissed her.

I don't want to kiss her. I want to ruin her, taint her good girl reputation. And I don't need to actually kiss her to do that. But fuck I want to kiss her. And taste her.

"*Fuck!*"

"What man? You bummed I whipped ya arse at duty again?"

"Huh? What?"

"You cursed out loud man."

"Oh shit, um nah. All good," I reply, shaking my head.

He pauses the game and glares at me.

"Not buying that. You're thinking about her, huh?

"Who? Fallon?" I ask, trying to get Zeke to back off.

"Oh yeah, pull my dick wanker. I'm talking about Tempany."

"Why would I be thinking about Tempany?" I question him, secretly loving how her name sounds rolling off my tongue.

"Because she's hot dufus. Don't tell me you don't want to root her?"

I chuckle. In my head, I have to admit to myself the idea of fucking Tempany isn't repulsive, but there's no way I'm going to let on to Zeke that's the case.

"Not in this lifetime. Have you forgotten that I hate her?"

He laughs at me. "Hate sex is the best kind."

"Oh, right. And you'd know that how?"

"Because I fucked Chasity Rogers, and I hate the shady bitch, but the sex was hot."

"Well, that's only because she's had the entire male school population inside her cunt. Any chick can be a good root if they've had enough practice."

"To right. So we going to Beau's party on Friday?"

"Might as well," I reply, turning my head to the archway when my little sister comes running in excitedly.

"Hey Av's. What's got you frothing?" I ask seeing the obvious excitement in her eyes. She runs into the room more, crashing against the back of the couch.

"Our new step sis and stepdad are coming over for dinner. Mum's been cooking all day."

"Oh, fuck, that's tonight?"

"Yeah, apparently she started school today, and her Dad wants to meet us straight away."

"Great," I mumble, glancing over at Zeke who's staring at Ava. His eyes are practically falling out of his head, and he licks his lips when Ava walks off.

"Damn," he curses under his breath. "When did your sister get so damn fuckable?"

My eyes boggle at him, and anger bubbles in my guts. I raise my hand, and slap my palm across his cheek.

"Fuck man, what you slapping me for?"

"For ogling Ava. She's my sister man. So tell ya dick to calm the fuck down."

"Come on Ash, you can't blame me for looking when she saunters into the room dressed all sexy."

I'm so pissed, the anger rushing through my veins. There is no way in hell I'd ever let my manwhore of a best mate anywhere near my fifteen-year-old sister.

"Fuck off you tosser! My sister and the word sexy do not belong in the same sentence!"

"Mmm, yeah, whatever. But Ava is fine man."

"Don't even start, Ezekiel," I taunt my best mate, using his full name because he hates it so much. "If you so much as even talk to her I'll fuck you up so bad, you won't be able to walk."

"Damn bro, chill, I won't touch her, fuck," he replies with a chuckle that turns my gut.

I love Zeke like a brother, so that's probably why the thought of him with my little sister turns me into a raging monster.

But being the male in the house—at least for now—it's my job to protect my sister.

And if I have my way she won't even look at a guy—especially my manwhore best mate—until she's thirty.

Zeke picks up my controller from the floor, giving me a smile and handing it to me.

"Sorry man. I'll keep my dick in my pants. Promise."

"You better, Ezekiel," I taunt pressing play to start a new game.

Seven

Tempany

*A*fter Ashton took my skirt in the change room, I put my dress back on, wipe an arm across my tear stained cheeks and head to my car.

I shouldn't be getting upset over his words, but his teasing hurts. I've done nothing wrong, and haven't seen him for ten years and he still seems to hate me.

I'm also upset with myself for the way my body reacts to Ashton. When he's near I feel tingly all over, straight into my damn knickers and I can't help but think about him touching me, kissing me and more.

The carpark is dead, only a few cars left when I walk out to my car—my cute little red Fiat 500 that dad bought me for my sixteenth birthday. Dad isn't made of money, but he spoils me; most likely to make up for all the time he lost not being to see me when I was younger.

Sometimes I'd wished I'd actually gone with him when he left Mum and Lockgrove Bay, but I didn't want to leave my friends. Little did I know that in less than a year I'd be doing that anyway. And life was hell because I'd stayed with Mum, her drinking, drug-taking and the revolving door of dead beat boyfriends.

Sliding into my baby, I shake the thoughts of Mum away, and wipe more tears away so my face isn't streaked with tears when I arrive home. Dad will already be wondering why I'm so late.

I drive through town, past the park by the beach and basketball court, and I wonder if Ashton still plays basketball there. He always seemed so happy and carefree when he was there, but now he's changed and seems fierier when it comes to basketball.

I should have gotten into sports more, but most of the time I preferred to hide in the library or the music room. Anything to not have to face the taunts and stares of my classmates, who knew all about my mum's wrongdoings. I was tainted with her reputation, her name, and it was best to hide from that.

Getting home I walk in the house to find Dad sitting at the kitchen bench, sipping a coffee whilst scrolling through his phone.

"Afternoon, honey," he greets me, smiling. "How was your first day?"

"Um, pretty good," I mumble, feeling the tears stinging my eyes again. "It was great seeing Lorena again."

"That's great honey. How are your classes?" he asks, taking a sip of his coffee before putting it down on the bench when he sees that I'm about to break into tears.

"Tempany, is something wrong honey?" he asks standing up.

"Well, it wasn't really the best day. A boy came into the change room's after P.E and took my netball skirt."

"Oh Tempany, that is horrible. What was he doing in the girls change rooms?"

"I um, don't know. But I don't have a netball skirt now."

"Don't worry about that. We'll get you a new one. Do you know this boys' name?"

I gulp, wondering for a moment if I should tell my dad 'yes'.

If Ashton finds out I snitched and cried to my dad he'll surely tease me more, and call me all matter of names. I decide to lie to my dad, even though he's clearly upset for me, and it feels beyond wrong to tell him lies.

"Um, no I don't know his name."

"Well, if he gives you any more trouble, please tell me honey, and I will speak to the school."

"Thanks, Dad," I reply, wrapping my arms around him in a hug.

"I love you Tempany," he tells me, kissing my hair and I smile.

"I love you to Dad."

Pulling back from the hug, he crosses the kitchen and puts his coffee cup in the sink, before he turns back to look at me.

"Are you going to wear that tonight?"

"Tonight? What for?" I ask confused.

"We're going to my new lady friends house for dinner. So we can meet her kids."

"Oh, I didn't realise that was tonight. I'll go get changed."

"Wonderful, honey. Take your time," he tells me before turning back to the sink of dishes, whilst I go upstairs to get changed.

I haven't unpacked all my clothes yet, but I know what I'm planning to wear.

From my suitcase, I pull out one of my favourite dresses. A blue tie-dye halter neck, with a handkerchief hem that sits just above my knees. I slip some gold bangles on, and change my earrings to some simple drop pendants, before pulling my hair up into a ponytail.

I slip on some black thongs, with diamente's on them, and run back downstairs to find Dad has changed as well into some chino shorts and a polo shirt.

"You look nice, Dad," I tell him.

"You look beautiful, honey. And to be quite frank, I'm nervous," he tells me with a soft chuckle.

"I'm sure it will be fine. She seems lovely from when we spoke on the phone. And you've met in person."

"That's true, so are you ready to go?"

"If you are," I reply smiling as we head out to Dad's Range Rover.

I climb in, and we drive towards the beach on the other side of town. I can't help but marvel at how the houses change from quant small townhouses like ours to huge elaborate mansions, right on the beach with big gates and intercoms.

Loathing Temptation

Dad pulls up in front of a beautiful white mansion, with huge windows and a large double stained glass front door.

I'm completely dumbstruck by the lavish house in front of me. It feels like I've stepped into another world, that I couldn't dream of ever being a part of.

I get out of the car, and Dad takes my hand, leading me up to the front door. He presses the doorbell, and the singsong sound reverberates through the house.

I can't help but wonder if they can hear it in the whole house when the door opens and a stunning blonde woman opens the door, looking at my Dad with a huge smile.

"Matias," she says with a sweet tone, pulling him into a hug, and kissing his cheek softly.

"I'm so glad you're here." She turns to look at me. "And you must be Te? My dear, you look beautiful."

"Thank you, um, Ms," I stammer, realising I don't know her name.

"Ms Castello, but please dear, call me Sascha."

Castello. Ashton's last name is Castello. Surely not.

"Come in, come in. My son is in the rumpus room, and my daughter will be down in a moment. Follow me."

We both follow her inside, and I take a moment to glance around the house, my eyes at first looking at the grand staircase before they spot two people in the rumpus room as we walk past to the dining room.

Sitting on the chaise, playing a video game is Ashton.

He looks right at me, dropping his controller.

His eyes flare with the same lustful look from earlier at school in the change rooms, and with more revealing clothes on I feel my whole body blush.

Ashton Castello is going to be my stepbrother.

This cannot be happening.

Eight

Ashton

Stepping into the room her eyes boggle at me, her whole body flushing when my gaze locks on her.

My temptress is in my house, looking sexy as fuck, but oh so innocent.

I lick my lips, staring her down, taunting her and waiting for her to bite. But instead, she turns on her heels, and clomps straight back out the door, with the slap of her thongs against her feet echoing around the room.

Her dad looks annoyed, turning his attention to me. "Hello again, Ashton. I'm sorry about my daughter. She's not normally so rude."

"Hello, Mr Davies. And it's fine. I'm sure Tem was just shocked to see me outside of school."

"Oh, so you know my Tempany?"

"You could say that. But we're not exactly friends and she's in year eleven," I tell him.

"Right yes," he replies, giving my mum a smile. "Sascha, I'm so sorry. I'll be back in a moment and can meet you in the dining room."

"No worries, darling," she tells Tem's dad with a sweet smile before she turns her attention to me.

"Ashton, dear. Will you go get your sister to come down, and be in the dining room in ten minutes?"

"No worries mum," I reply as she heads to the kitchen.

The smell of roast lamb is wafting out into the hallway, and it smells fucking delicious. Mum had always been a great cook, and her roast with all the trimmings, lashed with rich meaty gravy is my fave.

I stand up from the couch at the same time Zeke does.

He slaps me hard on the back, grinning.

"Shit man. It got real. And as much as I'd like to stay for this shit show I'm out. Catch ya at school."

My best mate walks out, leaving me still standing in the rumpus room, and processing what has just happened.

Tempany or Te, as she wants to be called now is going to be my new stepsister.

And I'm fucking cut.

And damn confused about what to do. I can't disappoint mum by being an arse to her, but my anger threatens to spill over every

Loathing Temptation

time I lay eyes on my temptress, not to mention the hard on's in my daks when I think about her.

I'm so fucking screwed and not in a good way.

I hate Te Davies. She still has the power to make my life hell and I fucking hate her for that and what she did ten years ago.

I can hear mum in the kitchen finishing off the food, and I'm about to head upstairs to get Ava to come down when she comes bounding down the stairs like she's as high as a kite.

Which is not possible.

My little sister is a nerd, popular but a nerd. Much like my temptress, who with her dad decides on that very moment to make her grand re-entrance to the house.

Ava bounds up to her, squealing. "Oh my god, hi...you're here. I'm Ava and you must be Te. You're so pretty." My sister wraps Tem into a hug, jumping up and down on the spot. And I pull her back, berating her, "Av's. Calm down yeah? You're not five."

"I know, Ash. But I can't believe how perfect this is."

Tem doesn't know where to look, and gives her dad and then me a shy smile when Ava takes her hand to lead her into the dining room.

She still seems angry, barely able to look at me. And I can't decide whether that's a good thing or not. It doesn't stop the anger in me and doesn't stop my dick trying to say hello at the front of my daks.

Mum comes out holding a dish of roast potatoes and I take it from her, heading into the dining room as Matias follows her into the kitchen. I put the dish on the table, and sit down across from

Caz May

Tem, staring at her. She completely ignores me, chatting away with Ava like they're besties.

Our parents come in then, putting the rest of the food on the table and Mum sits at the head of the table, Matias next to me.

The tension is so thick, you could cut it with a knife. I literally want the floor to swallow me whole. This is a hella awkward dinner, and absolute fucking torture.

We say grace, ending with Ava and I chanting out a bellowing, "Amen, amen. Oh, I said Amen, yeah."

I high five my little sister and we laugh. Mum smiles at Tem and Matias.

"They always do that as our ending to grace," she tells them, and a smile cracks the corner of Tem's lips. I hate that she's getting to see this side of me. The not so cocky Ashton that only my family gets to see. She's not my family, and she's not going to feel at home here.

She shattered my world ten years ago. And things haven't exactly been happy families since then, so she can go fuck herself.

Oh fuck me. She'd look sexy as sin riding me.

I shake the thoughts away, thinking of dead rodents to get my screaming dick to calm down. I'm sitting next to her father for fucks sake. And I've got a hard on, thinking about having dirty hot hate sex with his daughter.

"So dig in, plenty to go around." Mums voice breaks into my wicked thoughts and I start piling on food in heaps on my plate; slices of lamb, roast potatoes and green beans. I practically pour

Loathing Temptation

half the gravy over my plate and mum chastises me, "Ashton, please leave some for everyone else."

I decide to be a dick. She knows I love my gravy.

"Should have made more, mum."

She gives me parental dagger eyes, the how dare you eyes. "Don't be a brat, Ashton Oliver. We have guests."

Fuck, she hit me in the damn feels. Using the full name card against me. "Sorry mum," I reply, sheepishly giving her a smile.

"Thank you, dear, just mind your manners and language."

I nod and start to devour my pile of gravy and lamb. It tastes delicious and I moan, licking my lips and glaring at Tem at the same time.

She shifts uncomfortably in her seat, obviously pressing her tingling thighs together. She doesn't look at me, just slowly eats her food, putting her fork down with a clank against her plate when mum asks, "So Te, how was your first day back at Lockgrove prep?"

I stifle my laugh, trying not to choke on my food when Tem takes a deep breath in. I'm fully prepared for her to throw me under the bus, but she smiles at mum, sweetly.

"It was great. It was lovely to see my best friend Lorena again."

"Oh yes, Mayor Baker's daughter. Lovely girl."

"Yes, and all my classes are good. Excerpt for P.E being mixed with the year twelves this year," she tells mum, kicking me in the shin under the table.

Fuck shit. Fuck. God that fucking hurts.

"Oh, that's interesting," mum replies, turning to me. "Ashton dear, do you know anything about that?"

"No mum. Why would I know anything about that?"

"Haven't you talked to your father lately? He throws money at the school. Surely he could be in on them hiring more teachers."

"Well, no mum, I haven't seen daddy dearest lately. But I'll be sure to ask him to throw more money at *'my'* school so he can further fodder his hate for me and Av's."

She glares at me, but doesn't entertain my taunts, nor does she say anything else about my father. Talking about him at the dinner table isn't really the best of conversation anyway, and the shocked looks on Tem's and her dads face confirm that.

Speaking of her dad, he suddenly breaks his silence, "So Ashton, Ava, your mother and I were thinking it would be a lovely idea for you kids to go out for a day together. Get to know one another before the wedding."

My mouth falls open. In absolute shock. This is the first I'm hearing of a fucking wedding. Yeah, Tem's dad being with my mum kinda makes her my stepsister, but them getting married makes it official.

Sign, sealed and delivered.

Here Ashton, stepsister delivery. And guess what, you hate her.

"Excuse me?" I question, looking at my mother angrily. "Why is this the first time we're hearing about this wedding?"

"We wanted to wait and tell you, until tonight. It didn't seem right to do over FaceTime."

"Well, of course not. But springing it on us tonight isn't exactly right either," I taunt, emphasising the word right and air quoting it.

"Well, Ashton dear. I'm sorry, but it's happening. And I'd appreciate it if you'd pretend to be happy for me," my mum says sobbing.

Loathing Temptation

Matias reaches out to touch her arm, looking at her with so much love. I feel like the worst son ever.

"I'm sorry mum."

"I know Ashton," she replies, giving me a smile that tells me I'm only just forgiven. "Now be a dear and help me clean up."

I stand up, grabbing my plate and Matias'. I nearly trip over when Tem stands up the exact moment I walk past her chair.

"Would you mind telling me which way the bathroom is?" she asks, not really to any one of us in particular.

"Straight up the stairs, second door on the left," Ava replies, picking up her plate and handing it to me.

"Thanks," she says singsongy, heading up the stairs with her dress swishing from side to side.

Again as I'm heading to the kitchen I nearly trip and drop the plates because that dress is barely a scrap of fabric and I get a little flash of her white lace knickers that has my dick doing a dance in my daks.

I hate Tempany Davies. But fuck she gets to me in ways no stepsister should. My body clearly hasn't gotten the we hate Tempany message.

Traitorous fucker that Ash Jnr is.

Dropping the dishes in the kitchen sink I think about Zeke's words about fucking Tem. About fucking Tem before she's my stepsister, and it being dirty hot hate sex.

Ash Jnr certainly likes the idea of that and I'm beginning to as well. Because I'm now standing in my kitchen, semi hard for my temptress that I hate with a burning passion.

Nine

Tempany

Rushing up the stairs, I pass the first room which has the door shut so I presume it's Sascha's room.

Ashton's mum seems nice but private and I like that. Like that she seems like she's the complete opposite of what my mother was. She put her rude son in his place and I wanted to hug her and blurt out thanks and tell her everything her son did to me today.

The Castello home seems foreboding from the outside, a mansion that I couldn't dream of being in, but being inside it I feel welcome and after dashing to the bathroom, I can't help but wander down the landing hallway to see the other rooms.

Loathing Temptation

The bathroom, which was simple but stunning with black tap ware and a double open shower with a claw foot bath to finish it off is next to a room that also has a closed door. It's clear whose the room is because it has a pink sign with hearts on it that says, 'Ava's room'.

The next room is empty and my heart leaps in my chest wondering if it will be mine to decorate how I want. I'd never had my own room growing up, having slept on the sofa bed in the lounge room in mum's one bedroom dump of a house. It smelt like cat wee, and the blankets I'd had to wrap around me to keep warm had been full of holes and thin. I shiver thinking about bitterly cold nights of the past when she'd come in drunk or high and climb onto the sofa next to me. She'd yank the blanket away and clutch it tight sobbing like a wounded animal because one of her deadbeat boyfriends had again dumped her.

But the shiver I'm feeling now is also because I've reached the end of the landing hallway, and I'm standing in front of an open door. In front of a room that is clearly Ashton's.

It's messy, the double bed in the middle strewn with black sheets and a mink blanket with a basketball picture on it. The walls are covered in posters, of famous basket ballers—Shaquille O'Neil and Kobe Bryant—as well as pictures of half naked women draped over cars in compromising positions. I feel like a prude looking at them, but that's probably because I am.

I'd kissed a few guys, but that was all. No guy has ever really given me the time of day, and the few who have never stuck around after kissing me or when they found out my mother was the town whore. I was expected to put out because of who my mum was, and when I didn't I'd always been discarded and called names like a prude, and frigid little bitch.

I know I shouldn't but I step further into Ashton's room, intoxicated by the smell of him that permeates the space—earthy, and a mix of leather and chocolate chip cookies.

Some clothes are tossed on the floor by the bed, basketball shorts and a blue basketball guernsey. My mind wanders to seeing him in that with nothing on underneath, and I feel a tingle in my knickers. The same tingle I felt at the dinner table when he wouldn't stop staring at me whilst he ate. The way he licked his lips made me think again of kissing him. I shouldn't be having these feelings about Ashton. He's going to be my stepbrother, but something about him stirs up lust in my belly like I've never experienced before.

I'm about to pick up the guernsey to sniff it—stupidly—when I hear footsteps coming down the hallway. I rush out but I'm not quick enough and stepping out of his room I bump into Ashton, and he pushes me against the wall, his anger flaring in his cloudy grey-blue eyes.

Loathing Temptation

Ten

Ashton

After finishing the dishes I head upstairs, feeling off as though something is amiss. I'm fully aware that Tem didn't make an appearance after heading to the bathroom, and that was easily fifteen minutes ago. So unless she was doing a huge shit, she was snooping.

I creep down the hallway to my room, manoeuvring around the creaky floorboard so to not alert her to my presence. And just as I suspected when I reach my bedroom door, Tempany is in the middle of the room about to pick up my basketball guernsey.

I take a step back, so she doesn't see me. But she knows I'm there for sure. She rushes out and I pull her aside, pushing her against the wall outside my room.

Standing close to her—I glare into her stormy eyes—taunting her, "What were you doing in my room, temptress?"

Her breath hitches, her tits rising against my chest.

"Um, nothing. I...got lost."

"Oh really? Lost huh?"

"Yeah, I couldn't remember which way Ava said."

"Sure, Tempany. You were snooping. Admit it."

She mumbles something I can't understand, biting down on her plump lower lip, drawing my eyes from hers.

Fuck me.

Watching her bite her lip sends a jolt of electricity through my body, and fuck me, I want to kiss her. Kiss her and take her lip in between my teeth. I've practically got precum dripping out of my dick just thinking about it.

It's clear she's not going to respond, so I seethe at her, "If you set foot in my room again, Tem, mark my fucking words you'll regret it."

I take a step back, releasing her from my hold on her. Still staring daggers at her though, so she gets my point. I can hear her breathing, her deep breaths to calm herself. And before I can walk into my room she steps aside, placing one foot just inside my bedroom door as though she's deliberately trying to piss me off.

"Oh no, you fucking didn't, Temptress," I taunt, grabbing her waist and pulling her back again.

Her deliberate defiance has riled me up and the smirk on her face, I so badly want to kiss it off. She's like a walking wet dream, taunting me with her actions and with her outfit choice again.

Loathing Temptation

"Make me regret it, Ashton," she teases me, again biting her lip. I press my forehead and —panting—my lips just a breath from hers. I could kiss her, taste her, and make her want me, but I pull back, shoving her aside.

Not even looking back at her I walk into my room and slam the door. Leaning against it, I wait for her steps to retreat down the hallway—over the creaky floorboard—before I fall onto my bed in a heap.

If I hate Tempany so much, then why the fuck do I want her so bad?

I hate Tempany Davies, and I want to do bad things to her.

Eleven
Tempany

$\mathcal{A}$fter eating lunch, I drag Lorena into the library. I don't want to even look at Ashton, or have him staring at me like he wants to eat me.

I'd thought all night about him nearly kissing me. His lips were so close to mine, I could almost feel them and I wondered what actually kissing him would be like.

"Te, why are we going to the library?" Lorena asks as I push the double doors open, whilst dragging her inside.

"So I don't have to look at Ashton."

Loathing Temptation

"Something happen with you guys?" she asks wide eyed when she sits down on the couches in the middle of the main library space.

It's abuzz with people chatting, and others studying. I feel at home and sit down next to Lorena.

"I kinda got caught snooping in his room."

"Oh shit. Did he go off?"

"Yeah kinda, but he nearly kissed me."

"Oh damn. Why didn't you kiss him then instead?"

"Because he's going to be my stepbrother Lo. I shouldn't want to kiss him."

"So what if he's your stepbrother? You think he's hot. I say go for it."

"Yeah I think he's hot but I'm not sure. My dad would hit the roof if he found out."

Lorena sighs, as though she doesn't know what else to say, and she doesn't get to reply due to the bell ringing. I jump up from my seat—rushing out—and calling out to her, "I gotta get to drama, but meet me at my car after school."

Lorena is sitting on my bed, already dressed in a long sleeved leopard print dress that dips almost to her belly button, and skims the top of her thighs. She looks stunning with her dark chocolate hair down around her shoulders. She's put on a touch of makeup and has knee high socks on to wear with her tan thigh high boots.

"So are you going to make Ashton want you tonight?" She asks with a giggle.

"No, well, um I don't know," I reply shaking my head and stepping back from my wardrobe holding a dress in my hands.

"Ooo, that's a pretty colour," Lorena remarks, her eyes darting to the burgundy silk dress I'm holding.

"Turn around Lo," I tell her. She closes her eyes, and I pull off my denim shorts and t-shirt, slipping the dress over my head. It's long sleeved and flowy all the way to the floor.

"You can open your eyes, Lo."

She gapes at me. "Te, what the hell is that?"

"A pretty dress."

"That is the most hideous dress I've ever seen."

"I think it's nice," I reply with a smile, smoothing the fabric down at the front.

"For a grandma or someone with no figure to show off to sexy boys."

I gulp, annoyed at my best friend for her reaction.

"Maybe I don't want to show off my figure."

She laughs at me and it kinda hurts.

"Well, you've got one and you should Tem."

"Hmmm, well maybe another time. I'm comfortable wearing this and if you make me change it I'm not going to the party."

"Fine, wear it, but don't expect Ashton to give you a second glance."

"I don't want him to look at me. It makes me feel all tingly," I tell her blushing, and slipping my feet into some strappy maroon sandals to match the dress.

"You want him, Te. Admit it."

"You know I do. But nothing is going to happen between us."

"You don't know that," she replies, smirking at me and pulling on her boots.

"I do know, Lorena. He is my stepbrother. And he is off limits."

74

"Not yet he isn't," she teases, standing up and smoothing her dress down a little so the hem meets the top of her boots.

"Yeah, but will be, so I can't get involved with him because, in the end, I'll be heartbroken."

"Well, bestie I love you, but your loss," she teases again with a smirk. "So you ready for your first Lockgrove Prep party?"

"Ready as I'll ever be, but remember we have to be back by eleven."

"Yes, dufus. We will be back by eleven, even though the party will only just be starting then."

I grab my keys and phone, putting them in a black clutch with a shoulder strap. "Have you got your phone?" I ask Lorena worriedly. "Just in case we get separated."

She pats her boob. "In here, sweetie," she teases.

"Weird Lo, but ok. And I'm sorry about the curfew. My dad's rule of my curfew being the same as my school year level is pretty stupid."

"Yeah, let's go so we have some time to enjoy the party."

We walk out the front door, and I make sure I've locked it. Dad left an hour ago for his date with Ms Castello, and won't be home until late; hopefully well after eleven because I don't want to lie to him about where I've been.

I'm about to get into my car when Lorena grabs my hand, laughing.

"Tem, we're walking. Beau's house is around the corner."

"Oh, ok," I mutter stumbling along behind her as she drags me down the quiet street.

I'm feeling nervous, one because we're out walking the dimly lit streets of my neighbourhood at night, and two because we're going to a party where there is sure to be alcohol.

I've never drunk alcohol before, having seen the catastrophic consequences it had on my parent's marriage and also how it affected my mum in general. The whole house smelt of beer, and vomit that day I found her. And my stomach lurches just thinking about it.

"You ok, Te?" Lorena asks, stopping in front of a single storey weatherboard house. "You look pale."

"I'm fine. Let's just go inside, and get a drink or something," I say with a smile.

"Oh yeah," Lorena chants racing up the path to the front door and verandah.

She doesn't knock on the door—because no one would hear over the blaring techno music—and pushing it open she rushes inside.

And after only taking like two steps into the open plan house I see him. Ashton *'gorgeous as hell'* Castello, leaning against the kitchen bench sipping a drink from a red plastic cup. He looks absolutely amazing, black jeans that hug his toned legs, ripped at the knees and a white fitted t-shirt that's clinging to his abs and stretching over his body as he lifts the cup to his lips and lowers it again.

His eyes catch mine, and for a moment I'm frozen to the spot.

I need to get out of here before he's in my face again.

My dress feels like it's burning my skin, clinging to me and I want to rip it off. I grab Lorena's hand, nodding towards Ashton. "Go get him, girl," she taunts.

Loathing Temptation

"No, I'm just going to find the bathroom. Can you get me a coke to drink?"

"Sure, I'll come to find you," she replies, her tone flat as we part ways.

Heading down the hallway—looking for the bathroom—I feel like everyone is staring at me, but I know only one person is.

And I'm cursing myself for ever agreeing to come to this party, knowing he'd be here.

Twelve

Ashton

Grabbing a cup of beer from the bench, I lean against it, scanning the room.

The lounge room is full of people grinding on each other, dry humping to the techno music that is pulsing throughout the speakers around the room. Beau doesn't live in the richest part of town, and from the outside, his house looks like a quaint beach shack, but inside it has every bell and whistle, including wall speakers in every room.

I take a sip of my beer, peering out over the rim.

"Dipshit, don't tell me you're looking for Tem?"

"Of course not," I retort to my best mate. But the truth is *'Yes'* I'm looking for my temptress. I know the party thing probably isn't her scene, but everyone comes to Beau's parties.

"Right, so you going to get with someone else tonight then?" Zeke asks elbowing me in the side.

"Nope," I reply, popping the p, and taking another sip of beer when I feel the cool evening air rush in from the front door opening.

And I shiver—not from that—but from who has entered the house.

I take another sip of beer, gulping it down hard and gripping the bench behind me when our eyes lock on each other.

She panics, nodding at me and saying something to Lorena before walking away.

Zeke senses my unease. "You ok man?"

"Um yep fine. Just felt a chill."

"Really or you got tingles because your girl just walked in?"

"Tem is not my girl, Zeke."

He laughs at me, a deep belly laugh that grates on my nerves.

"I didn't say Tem man. You did."

"Fuck off, idiot. I'm not near drunk enough to deal with your shit tonight."

"Someone's got his knickers in a twist. And you love me."

I grab another cup of beer, gulping half of it down whilst I think of a witty remark to say back to Zeke.

"I'm commando, dude."

"Um, yep, ripper," Zeke replies, licking his lips. I want to chunder from that reaction, but see his eyes set on Lorena walking

79   Caz May

up to us. Her outfit screams come and get me boys, and Zeke the manwhore is taking her bait.

"Hey boys, is there anything to drink besides beer?"

Zeke's eyes are practically falling out of his damn head. And he's clearly not able to form a sentence so I look to Lorena and reply, "Beer or water."

"Great, thanks, Ashton." She gives me a wink and steps past Zeke towards the fridge.

"You gonna crack a fat man?"

He shakes his head. "Fuck, man. Lorena is smoking tonight."

"Whatever you say. But maybe keep your tiny dick in your daks tonight. The school year has only just started."

"Not a chance. But hey, she might not be down for a ride on the Z-train."

Lorena comes back, clutching a bottle of water. "Nice seeing you both, I'll catch you later after I give this to Tem."

I raise an eyebrow at the mention of my temptress. And before I can think otherwise I offer, "I'll take it to her. Ezekiel here needed to ask you something."

Her eyebrow raises at me questioningly but she hands the bottle of water to me with a smirk.

Zeke gives me a slap on the back, a non-verbal thank you and I walk away, clutching the water bottle in a fist.

Just the thought of running into Tem is making my whole body hot with lust.

I'm about to give up on finding her when she steps out of the bathroom, smoothing down her hideous burgundy dress.

It hides her body and looks like something from the worst pile of hand me downs ever. It's like one big scrap of ugly fabric.

She's not looking where she's going, so I purposely bump straight into her.

"Seriously, Tempany," I blurt out, shoving her back against the bathroom door. It opens and she stumbles back into the small room. She looks like she's about to cry, and I cage her against the counter, kicking the door closed.

"Here," I grunt, shoving the water bottle against her chest.

Big fucking mistake on my part. She inhales and I practically cop a feel of her tit beneath the thin fabric of her dress.

"Um thanks," she mutters, unscrewing the lid and taking a sip. "How come you brought me a drink? I asked Lorena to."

I laugh. "Lorena is otherwise occupied," I taunt, grabbing her waist and a fist of the dress. "Plus I wanted to see if this dress was just as hideous up close."

She arches her back, trying to let up my grip on her.

"It's not hideous," she barks out before taking her lip between her teeth.

"Temptress, it's heinous. It looks like you're wearing a potato sack."

"Does not. It's not even the same colour."

Again I laugh, gripping the fabric harder before yanking it back. The fabric rips, leaving the creamy skin of her hips exposed.

"Whoops," I jeer, stepping back from her and opening the door. She doesn't move for a moment, but I can hear her crying.

Back out in the main part of the house, I can see Zeke with Lorena. Their lips are locked together, their bodies almost one except for the clothes between them.

My best mate is such a manwhore. I can't help but think about his words, about finding someone to hook up with tonight, but truth be told I only want my temptress and right now—or maybe not at all—I can't have her.

Especially when she comes into the room, a hand trying to hold her dress together with an angry look on her face. She seethes at me, rushing up to Lorena and grabbing her arm.

I can't hear the words she's saying, but Lorena breaks her kiss with Zeke and looks at Tempany begrudgingly.

Tempany takes her hand and drags Lorena away, straight out the door without even a glance back to me.

Zeke comes back over to me, all chuffed like he's won the damn lottery.

"So did you rip that hideous dress whilst you nailed her?"

"No, didn't even kiss her," I admit. *'But fuck do I want to.'*

"Yeah, don't blame ya man. I bet her kisses would be ripe."

Fuck.

"I totally just said that out loud yeah?"

"Yeah, man. You want to kiss her, so grow some balls and do it."

"Yeah, so you just kissed Lorena? Or you got a little handsy?"

He blushes. Zeke actually blushes.

"Copped a feel, and got some hot pashes. And if Tem hadn't so rudely interrupted, my dick would have been going for an exploration under that short arse dress."

"Good thing you got interrupted then. Lorena doesn't need to see your tiny dick."

"You know my dick isn't tiny man."

"I know, just messing with ya. But being honest, I think you need to focus on school this year, not pussy."

"Seriously, dude. Are you alright?"

I shake my head, heading over to grab another beer.

"Not really. Dad is on my back again about my grades this year, and I don't want to let the tosser down."

"Fair point. Your old man is a hard arse."

"That's putting it nicely," I reply, gulping down the beer.

"Yep," Zeke replies gulping down his own beer. "Let's just get shitfaced. We don't have practice or a game tomorrow."

"Sounds ripper," I reply, grabbing a bottle of whiskey that's appeared on the bench. I unscrew the lid, and scull it, loving the burn as it slides down my throat.

I pass the bottle to Zeke, sighing and cursing out loud.

"Fuck, I just remembered I'm supposed to be taking Tem and Ava out tomorrow for some family bonding time. I'll um…" I cut my words off, rushing out the door to my Camaro.

I seriously hate Tempany, and I can't think of anything worse than having to spend a day with her.

Ok, I can think of worse things, like getting a beating from dad, but still.

I'll just have to make the most of it and find some way to make sure I can turn a horrible day into something that will ruin sweet Tempany.

Thirteen

Tempany

*G*etting home, I'm glad it's before eleven and Dad is not home yet.

The night air has become quite chilly and both Lorena and I are shivering.

Quickly I unlock the front door, putting my keys on the hallway table and heading straight to my bedroom with Lorena following me. The moment we step into my bedroom, she starts undressing. "Lo, what're you doing?" I ask, shocked at my best friend.

"Getting into PJ's. I'm freezing my tits off."

"Oh um...cool. I just don't want to see you naked." I stumble on the word naked.

Loathing Temptation

I don't really cover up completely with some of my outfits—like the dress I wore to Ashton's the other day—but being naked has always been shameful to me. It's probably because I always see *'his'* black eyes gazing over my body, and hear him telling me all sorts of things that a man shouldn't say to a child.

Depraved things, sexual things.

I shake my head, a grave disturbing shiver rushing through me.

Lorena chuckles. "Oh um...sorry."

"It's ok," I reply with a nod, rushing out of the room to turn the heater on. It seems stupid to be turning it on at the end of January but I'm deathly cold.

Heading back into my room, Lorena is now in a pink long sleeved t-shirt nightie, sitting on my bed with her legs crossed.

I grab out some pyjama shorts, hitch my dress up and slip them up my legs. Turning around I pull my dress off over my head, leaving my bra on.

Lorena's eyes lock on my discarded dress on the floor at my feet.

"What happened to your dress?"

"Ashton ripped it."

She smiles at me cheekily. "When? Did things get dirty when he bought you the drink?"

"No, things did not get dirty, Lo."

"Then what happened, Te? He clearly upset you."

I sit down next to her, pulling my knees up to my chest and resting my head on them.

"He pushed me against the sink and told me the dress looked like a potato sack," I tell her, rocking back and forth a little.

"And then what? He was kinda right about the dress, Te, but you didn't listen to me."

"He grabbed it in a fist and ripped it," I admit. "I don't know why he's being so mean."

Lorena smiles cheekily. "He's an arsehole Te, but he's so hot." I don't respond, and she pokes me playfully.

"And I think he wants you. He's not like that with other girls."

Her words make me feel defensive and I feel like yelling at my best friend for pushing me towards Ashton.

"Well, he might be hot. But I hate him and he's my soon to be live in stepbrother."

She laughs then. "You don't hate him. You love him," she taunts me.

"I...um...don't know what I feel for him. But it's certainly not love, Lorena."

"Keep telling yourself that, Tempany."

I bite down on my lip, processing my best friends words. And hate admitting that she's kinda right.

I feel something for Ashton I shouldn't. But there is something about him that gets to me, even though it's wrong. And after my experiences from the past and more recently with my mum's supposed boyfriends, I shouldn't want to feel or do anything remotely sexual. But I've thought about those things with Ashton.

Not that I'll admit that to Lorena or anyone else.

My little secret.

Fourteen

Ashton

Flipping the seat forward, I watch Tem awkwardly climb into the backseat of my Camaro.

She's wearing only a lace dress over her black bikini and I can't help but stare. Seeing her baring so much skin is turning me on. And getting in the driver's seat I adjust Ash Jnr in my board shorts when Ava plops into the front seat eyeing me like she knows I was just playing with my dick.

"So where are we going?" Ava squeals, practically deafening me.

"Well, considering how Tem is dressed, clearly the beach."

"Oh yes," Ava again screeches.

I'm glad the beach is only a short drive, as I don't think I could take much of hearing my sister excitedly chatting to Tempany.

Ava turns her head back to Tempany in the backseat.

"Te, I'm so glad you're going to be my sister. Like mega excited. I always wanted a sister."

"Seriously Av's, calm the fuck down," I chastise, looking back at Tem in the backseat in the rear vision mirror. She shifts uncomfortably in her seat.

"I...um...always wanted siblings too."

"Yeah, well some of us have enough siblings," I taunt Tem, her eyes catching mine again. She gulps, and I lick my lips, squirming a little in my seat when we pull up to the beachside carpark.

Ava gets out, flipping the seat back so Tempany can get out. I wait until they're both out the car before I get out.

Tempany walks off, down to the foreshore. And my gaze follows her, staring at the way her bikini rises up her arse cheeks as she walks. I know I shouldn't be looking at her, but I can't stop staring.

Ava is still standing beside me, and I jeer at her, "Why are you bugging me brat? Go play house with your new sister."

She slaps me in the ribs.

"You're being a dufus. I can see you staring at her."

"I'm not staring, Av's."

"Sure you aren't. You think Te looks hot."

"Her name is Tempany. Don't entertain her Te crap, Ava."

"Why are you being such an arse to her, Ash?"

"I'm not going to tell you why Ava. You don't need to know why I hate Tempany."

Loathing Temptation

"Whatever, brother. But I don't get why you're staring at her if you hate her so much."

I don't reply to that, checking that I have my phone in my board shorts pocket.

I probably shouldn't do what I'm planning but I still want to ruin her, so I follow Ava down to the beach, where Tempany is lying on her back on her towel.

She's stripped off the lacy barely there excuse for a dress, and her tits look perfect—hand size mounds—in the black triangle bikini top. If Ava wasn't still standing next to me, pulling off her shorts and t-shirt I'd have yanked Tem's bikini top off to see her bare tits. I'm fucking almost hard just thinking about it.

"Te, are you coming swimming?" Ava asks.

Tem's eyes flutter open, and she sits up.

"Maybe in a bit," she replies to my sister with a smile.

I yank off my t-shirt and lay down on the warm sand. Tem lays back down beside me, and I swear the sand beneath me sets fire. She again closes her eyes. And shocks me when she softly says, "I can feel you staring at me, Ashton."

"In your dreams, Tempany."

She lets out a little chuckle, and her tits bounce a little, making my dick jolt in my shorts. The temptation to strip her of the bikini and touch her everywhere is overwhelming, and only the fact we're on a public beach on a Saturday afternoon stops me.

At least that's what I'm telling myself when I pull my phone out of my pocket, sitting up and sneakily taking some pics of her in her bikini.

Caz May

She moans, rolling over onto her stomach, and I again snap a pic, this time of her arse. Because fuck me does she have a sexy arse.

Ash Jnr is jumping around in my board shorts, and I adjust him a little and lay back down again. This time I lay on my side, my face so close to Tem's I could kiss her. Her eyes flutter open and she gasps.

"What the hell, Ashton?" she screeches, shrinking back from me.

"What temptress?"

"Were you going to kiss me?" she asks, biting down on her lip.

"No, why would I want to kiss you?"

"Um, I...um..." she mutters, standing up and running into the surf.

I lift my phone, quickly taking a video.

Why does she have to be so fucking gorgeous?

And not even know it?

Twenty minutes later, after the girls are practically drowned rats we pull up to the park. Ava had insisted she wanted ice cream from the Frosty boy van that's always at the edge of the park in summer.

But to get to the van from the carpark we need to cross the basketball court, the very court I was playing on ten years ago when Tempany ruined my life. I've avoided this court for ten years —going to the other one out of my way on the other side of town —to avoid the memories of playing with Tempany, and what came after.

Loathing Temptation

My heart is hammering in my chest and I can't look at Tempany, afraid I'll crack and lash out at her. I'm halfway across the court, taking longer than necessary strides to not prolong the torture when I hear her voice. "Hey, I found a ball lying around. You down for a game, Ashton?" I stop dead in the middle of the court, heart hammering still when I turn to find Tempany standing in the middle of the court bouncing a basketball in between her legs.

Fuck me dead.

Stepping into her personal space and stealing the ball from her, I bounce it right up to the hoop before slam dunking it and hanging off the hoop for a moment. Her eyes don't leave mine for a second. I strip from my shirt, throwing it aside, and bounce the ball until I'm back in Tem's personal space.

Her eyes shine with something, lust, anger and a come hither look, plus they betray her by scanning my half-naked torso.

I find my voice, "You telling me you're down for a bit of two on one, Tem?"

"Oh, you bet, Ash. Ava and I are going to bring you down," she taunts, glancing at my little sister who is standing on the side of the court, a little lost.

"Av's, get over here sis."

Ava runs over, and I start dribbling the ball again, backing away from Tempany with every bounce. She's teasing me, steady steps side to side, as though she's waiting for the moment to strike. She steps closer, her hand between us, about to slap down on the ball.

"Don't steal my ball temptress," I taunt her, grinning.

Annoyance flashes in her eyes when I rush off, shooting for an easy goal. Before I can catch the rebound, Ava intercepts it laughing and bouncing the ball back to Tem.

Tem glares at me and laughs when she speaks, "I'd never steal your ball, Ashton. Here!" I don't have a moment to think about her words because she throws the ball at me, straight into my nuts. Ash Jnr throbs.

I'm in agony, and I scream out, "Fuck Tem! You trying to kill me."

Her and Ava are both laughing like kookaburras, and I'm clutching my aching nuts. I want to tear her damn hair out, or kick her in the twat.

"No, I was trying to bring you to your knees, Ashton."

"Well, fuck you, Tempany," I curse her out, angrily before huffing and sauntering off awkwardly, still clutching my nuts.

Tempany is going to pay for this. Seriously I don't know who she fucking is anymore.

One minute she's sweet, shy, and takes my taunts, the next she's spitting out innuendo and bringing me to my knees.

And now—albeit awkwardly—walking across the park, only the fact that Ava is with us is stopping me from heading back to Tempany and taking out my anger—my hatred of her—with a kiss that would have us both on our knees.

Fuck, now I'm going to have blue balls too.

Being around Tempany Davies is dangerous.

I need to avoid her, ignore her or I'll be on my knees with her clutching my damn balls.

Loathing Temptation

Fifteen

Tempany

Ashton storms off, in a rage and clutching his crotch. I feel bad for throwing the ball at him, especially because I deliberately went for his crotch to hurt him.

I'm about to chase after him to apologise when Ava hip bumps me.

I turn to look at her and she's grinning.

"What?" I ask sheepishly.

She giggles, before asking, "Are you crushing on my brother?"

My eyes boggle at her.

"No, of course not. Why would you think that?"

"Because you can't stop staring at him."

"I don't stare at Ashton."

"Whatever sis," Ava taunts, elbowing me again.

I open my mouth to reply, but words are caught in my throat. Partly because Ava just called me sis, but mainly because she's right about my crushing on Ashton.

I want to hate him as he hates me, but I can't. He makes me feel giddy, and I crave the moments I have with him when he's taunting me, as stupid as that is. Butterflies fill my stomach and tingles erupt all over my body when I'm near Ashton.

And I hate that, not him.

"So sis, tell me about yourself?"

"Not much to tell," I reply laughing and heading across the basketball court in the direction Ashton went.

Ava follows, giggling when she asks, "What's your fave things?"

"Oh um, colour, pink, food, Margherita pizza, and ice cream flavour, caramel mud cake."

"Ooo, nice. I love pizza as well, and blue is my favourite colour."

I smile at her.

"I get the sense you're a bit of a tomboy."

"No not really, but I'm not into a lot of girly stuff like makeup, but dresses are my fave thing to wear."

"Cool, so um, are you crushing on anyone?" I ask, again giving her a sweet smile.

"I'll tell you, if you promise not to tell anyone, especially Ashton."

I burst out laughing.

"Why would I tell Ashton?"

Ava glares at me, holding her pinky up to me. "Pinky swear you won't tell my brother."

I link my finger with hers.

"I won't tell Ashton, I swear."

"Good. And um...I'm crushing so hard on Ezekiel."

"What? Seriously Zeke? As in Ashton's best friend?" I spit out.

"Yes, that Ezekiel. And if Ashton finds out, he'll be so mad."

"Why? Does Zeke like you back?"

"I don't know. Probably not. He's a player, and I know I shouldn't like him, but he's so gorgeous."

"Um, yeah, he's ok," I reply, biting on my lip.

Ava again glares at me and laughs again.

"You so are crushing on my brother, Te. If you don't think Ezekiel Alessio is hot, then you don't have eyes or have eyes for someone else."

"I'm not looking for a boyfriend. I need to focus on school."

"Well, Ashton is available. He just broke up with his bitch of a girlfriend, Fallon."

"Yeah, I heard about that. What happened?"

"They were together for two years. But I think she cheated on him. I never liked her anyway."

"Yeah, why's that?"

"She never wanted anything to do with me. I was just Ashton's annoying little sister."

"Sorry about that. Maybe his new girlfriend will be nicer."

"Yeah, I think she is," Ava replies with a smirk, stepping up behind Ashton who's sitting at a picnic table licking an ice cream.

My mind wanders to kissing Ashton, wondering what it would feel like to have his tongue in my mouth. Thinking that about him is so wrong.

I'm broken from my naughty thoughts when Ava asks, "Te, do you want ice cream?"

"No thanks. I'm good."

Ashton stands up, stepping up to me.

"Good, I wasn't planning on getting you one anyway."

My heart sinks with the malice in his tone, even when he turns to Ava and says to her, "Av's get it in a fucking cup. I don't want ice cream everywhere in the Camaro."

"Fine," Ava snaps at Ashton before ordering her ice cream.

I don't dare look at Ashton as we head back across the basketball court to his car.

He's still grumpy, and I'm too scared to apologise to him about throwing the ball at him.

He doesn't deserve my apology anyway. And despite my feelings for him—that are clearly one sided—I'm going to treat him how he treats me.

There's a fine line between love and hate.

Loathing Temptation

Sixteen

Ashton

Sliding under the bleachers into one of our usual spots—when we're not playing basketball—at lunch Zeke glares at me before taking a huge bite out of his sandwich.

He's still chewing—his mouth full—when he blurts out, "You never told me about what happened at the dinner?"

I gulp. "Well, Tempany practically threw me under the damn bus. And our parents decided we had to go out on the weekend to get to know each other."

"Bet that sucked?"

"Big time. I caught Tem snooping in my room after dinner too."

"Ooo, she was probably sniffing ya jocks."

"Yeah, dirty bitch," I reply with a laugh, thinking for a moment about the dirty things I want to do to Tempany. "But now after the weekend, I'm ignoring Tem."

I take a bite of my own sandwich, waiting for something else witty to come out of Zeke's mouth, but he's silent. The only sound is him munching on his sandwich like a cow.

I pluck my phone out of my pocket, sure that it had vibrated, but there's no message. I open the pictures of Tem I took on the weekend, wondering if I should show Zeke and tell him my plan to blackmail Tem with them. But I just lick my lips, staring at the pictures and thinking of how I nearly kissed her.

Zeke breaks me from my dirty thoughts, snatching my phone from my fingers.

He looks at the screen, chuckling.

"Ignoring her huh? Dipshit!" he jeers, still glaring at the pictures when I snatch my phone back.

"Well, I'm not talking to her, am I?" I question, rhetorically but Zeke still bites back.

"No, but you're staring at sexy pics of her. You catching feelings?"

I scoff. Then gulp hard to swallow the lump in my throat, before I reply, "Feelings? For Tem?"

"Nah, for the fucking postman," Zeke replies, cacking himself laughing. "Of course for Tempany, dufus."

I shake my head; at least I think I shake my head.

"Not in a million fucking years. Did you forget I hate her?"

Zeke again laughs, annoyingly.

Loathing Temptation

"So you keep saying, but actions speak louder than words my man."

"Whatever, dickwad. Couldn't have her even if I wanted to. She's going to be my stepsister in like a month."

"Yeah, that sucks balls man. You really should fuck her before that. Go after the hot hate sex."

If I still had any sandwich to chew in my mouth I'd have spat it at him.

"Fat chance. I'm not fucking Tempany."

Shockingly loud, Zeke blurts out, "Why the hell not? You need to get ya dick wet again man. You've not gotten any pussy since you broke up with Fallon."

He's right, and I hate that he's right, but I don't want anyone but Tempany. I'm just not going to tell Zeke that. He'd heap shit on me, even more than he is right now.

"Yeah, I know. I'm steering clear of all chicks though. To much fucking work," I tell him.

It's not completely untrue. Chicks are to much work. It takes to much to make them happy, but I don't think Tempany is that kinda girl.

I think back to the weekend and how she was so sweet and nice to Ava. And then not getting an ice cream. I'd said I wasn't going to pay for it if she'd wanted one, but I would have.

Mum would've slapped me about the head if she found out I was deliberately mean to Tempany on our day out.

Zeke looks like he's deep in thought as well. I slap his leg.

"Are you getting any pussy? Or are chicks to much work?"

"Yeah, way too much work, but some don't mind just rooting though."

"Yeah, who are you sinking your dick into?" I jeer with a chuckle.

"A good boy doesn't fuck and tell," he informs me, sniggering.

"You're not a good boy, Zeke," I tease him, laughing so hard I have to hold back a snort.

"True, but my lips are sealed."

I see red.

"It better not be my sister. I'll fucking kill you."

He laughs, and I want to throttle him. He's clearly got a jones for my little sister, and if he's touched her he's a fucking dead man walking.

"Nah, I wanna fuck Ava of course, but I'm not doing anything illegal. I'm not that stupid." I can't believe the words that have just exited his mouth. He's so dead.

"You sure about that?" I taunt because as much as I love him, Ezekiel Alessio is not the sharpest tool in the shed.

"Dead sure," he replies, nodding.

"So who are you rooting then?" I ask, gazing around the schoolyard to see if any chicks are staring us down more so than usual today.

"Lorena," he admits, proudly puffing his chest out. "We fucked in the change room after P.E yesterday."

I'm shocked and kinda annoyed.

"You fucked Tem's best friend?"

"Yeah, and she was a ripper root," he chortles, clearly thinking about it again. "I'd take her for a ride again if she's down."

"You fucking root rat," I jeer, laughing.

Loathing Temptation

"You love me," he teases, winking at me suggestively. "So when are you fucking Tem again? You know so we can compare them since they're besties."

I scoff, and then reply, "How about this side of never, and up yours Ezekiel!" I taunt, standing up.

The bell sounds as I walk off, leaving my best mate dumbfounded. Heading to class I'm thinking about Tem, wondering if she is a ripper root and wondering if she talks about sexual things with Lorena.

I do love Zeke. He's loyal and has always had my back, especially recently with the whole Fallon pregnancy disaster, but sometimes I wished my best mate could be more serious.

I want to share how much Tem is getting to me, but he'll just make a joke of it, tell me to fuck away my feelings. I'm not sure if that's even possible.

I hate Tempany, but that's not all I feel for her.

And Zeke would never understand that.

I'm fucked.

Seventeen

Tempany

Wednesday lunchtime and I'm avoiding everyone—again —including Lorena. She'd been bugging me all week about my day out with Ashton and Ava, and I don't know what to tell her.

The whole day, especially when we were at the beach has been playing on my mind. I was sure he was going to kiss me, and then he didn't.

His words of rejection hurt, and I hate that they do.

I don't want Ashton to hate me. I don't know what I want him to feel for me, but loathing isn't it for sure.

Loathing Temptation

I want to stop thinking about him—about him nearly kissing me again—but I'm reading my new fave authors latest release, *'Not my Girl'*,leaning against the stacks at the very back of the library. And it's giving me all the feels and I'm imagining Ashton as the main character.

It's frustrating that I can't get my stepbrother off my mind because I shouldn't want him for the very fact that he will be related to me in a month.

Dad also dropped the bombshell on me, on Sunday that we're moving into the Castello's mansion next weekend. I didn't want to act like a spoilt brat, and not be excited by that news but I honestly wanted to stomp my foot and throw a tantrum. It's not going to do anything and Dad means well. He's in love, and I'm happy for him.

I'm happy about having Ava as a little sister, but an older brother is not high on my Wishlist, especially one as infuriating and gorgeous as Ashton.

I can't really concentrate on reading so standing up I brush off my butt, clutch my book against my chest and start to head out of the library, sneakily.

I don't even make it to the end of the non-fiction aisle before Lorena corners me.

"Hey, girl. I thought I'd find you here."

My best friend knows me too well, the old me. And I curse myself for being so damn predictable.

"Um yeah, I was just reading, but I need to go to the dunny before class."

"Are you ok? You've been off all week."

She follows me as I head out of the library to the toilets down the corridor.

"Te, I asked if you're ok?" She pleads as we head into the toilets.

"I'm fine," I snap, going into a cubicle and putting my book on the floor.

I quickly pull my knickers down from under my skirt and curse, *'oh damn'* when I sit down on the dunny. My period has started and I don't have a tampon.

"Lo?" I call out. "Are you still there?"

"Yeah, Te. Are you going to talk to me or what?"

"I um...need a tampon. My period just started."

"Oh shit, um..." Lorena mutters. "Do you have any money on you?"

"No, why would you ask that?" I call out over the cubicle, yanking a copious amount of toilet paper out and shoving it haphazardly into my knickers.

I pull them up and hobble out of the cubicle.

Lorena laughs at me.

"Did you just put toilet paper in your undies?"

"What do you think? Not like I have any other option right now," I tell her, quickly washing my hands.

I eye the vending machine on the wall, as does Lorena.

"That's why I asked if you had any money, but maybe if we press the button and bash the shit out of it, we might get lucky."

I feel really guilty for what I reply, but I'm also desperate. "Worth a shot I guess."

"Ok, you press the button and I'll bash it," Lorena suggests.

I press the button, and Lorena bashes the side, rocking the vending machine until a packet of tampons slips out into the tray.

"Oh thank gosh," I mutter, grabbing them and rushing back into a cubicle.

Quickly I do my business, and come out, washing my hands and smoothing down my skirt.

"Thanks, Lo."

"No worries," she replies following me out to our lockers when the bell rings.

"Um, Te, I need to tell you something."

"Yeah, what?" I ask grabbing my sheet music for music out of my locker.

Lorena is standing next to me, standing against the lockers.

"I um...I..."

I look at her and can see her anxiousness. There isn't time for whatever conversation we need to have.

"Lo, I have to get to music class. Can you wait to tell me on the weekend at Ashton's?"

"Yeah, ok," she mutters with a smile.

I head to music class, with a weight on my shoulders. Something is up with Lorena, and I'm dreading the weekend; moving into Ashton's house.

Hopefully, music class will make me feel better, as it usually does. But my heart falls to the floor when I walk into the classroom and find Zeke sitting at a table clutching an electric guitar against his chest.

He looks up at me, a smirk on his face.

"Hey Tem, you here to get down?"

"Um, I'm here for class."

"Choir girl, huh?"

I step into the room, our teacher Mr Samuels right behind me in a mad hurry. I really want to turn out the door, to escape Zeke's eyes boring into me like he can see right through me. He doesn't get to me in the same way Ashton does, but Zeke still gets under my skin.

The room fills with other students, and I'm pushed further into the room, right into a seat next to Zeke.

He lifts his guitar over his head and puts it on the table in front of him. He leans into me.

"You could've told me you wanted to sit in my lap, Tem."

I glare at him.

"I um...don't want to do that."

He winks at me, smirking when he taunts, "Oh I know Tem. You only want to sit on Ashton's lap."

I scoff, but my stomach flip flops at the thought of sitting in Ashton's lap. Zeke breaks my thoughts, again taunting me, "Your lack of words tells all, Tem."

I turn my focus to Mr Samuels who's muttering something up the front of the room, shuffling sheet music.

"Ezekiel, did you prepare that song over the holidays for the eisteddfod?"

"You bet I did, Mr S. But I need a female lead."

He looks to me. And I gulp.

"Oh yes. Any volunteers?" Mr Samuels asks, his eyes scanning the room. They lock on me. "New student?"

"Yes, Mr Samuels."

"Please come up and introduce yourself."

I get to my feet, moving slowly up to the front of the room.

Loathing Temptation

I hear someone wolf whistle.

And turning around Zeke is glaring at me, all suggestively.

"Hi, everyone. I'm Te Davies. And I love to sing and perform."

Zeke hollers, "Oh yeah Tem!"

"Well, Miss Davies, I think it might be perfect to start with you singing Ezekiel's song."

Oh, holy Moses!

"Um ok, I guess," I mutter.

Zeke gets to his feet, grabbing his guitar again and sauntering up to the front of the room. He hands me a piece of paper with lyrics on it. And leans into whisper into my ear, "Go with it Tempany. Think of Ashton."

He starts playing a melody, whilst the drummer starts a beat.

I open my mouth to sing the lyrics, and I get lost in them.

Maybe music class won't be so bad.

Eighteen

Ashton

Again Zeke and I are sitting under the bleachers. It's a great spot to keep our eyes on everyone, but far enough away that we can talk shit about everyone and not have listening ears or lip readers. No one dares to come near us when we sit there, except for one person.

She saunters up to the bleachers, swaying her hips like she's trying to be seductive. What I saw in her, I really don't know now. Just looking at her coming towards me is enough to make bile rise in my throat, my lunch threatening to make another appearance.

She comes up to me, wrapping her arms around me. I push her away harshly and Zeke glares at me, chuckling under his breath.

Loathing Temptation

I wanna fucking punch him for being an arse. He mentioned her name moments ago, and the she devil, she appears.

She's still standing in front of me, clearly not getting the message that she's not welcome to breathe the same air as me anymore.

I'm about to open my mouth to tell her where to go—or to suck a dick other than mine—when she leans forward, pushing my back against the bleachers and crashing her lips to mine.

I wanted to chunder before, but now I literally have bile in my mouth. Gulping it down I bite down hard on Fallon's lip. She screeches, pulling back, and wiping an arm across her lip which is bleeding.

"What the hell, Ash?" She screams at me, tears stinging her eyes.

I laugh, standing up and pulling her up with me, with a fist full of her jumper.

"What don't you get Fallon?"

She mumbles something incoherent, licking the bite mark I made on her lip.

"I don't fucking want you anymore. Rack off!"

I let go of her jumper, shoving her away, and she walks off in a huff. Zeke laughs, clutching his stomach because he's in stitches.

"Damn, bro," he jeers, poking me in the arm. "You should put she devil in her place. That was brutal."

I snigger, an idea to get back at her ticking over in my mind. Revenge is sweet.

"Yeah I have an idea," I tell him, laughing when I think back to the last time Fallon sucked my dick. She's going to regret the choice she made that day.

"Ooo do tell," Zeke requests.

"Wait and see brother," I reply, still sniggering from how grouse the idea is.

Fallon is going down.

The Next day, clutching a pile of freshly printed flyers against my chest, I sneak into school way to early for any sane person to be entering the school building.

The crazy—possibly serial killer—janitor is the only person around at this ungodly hour, and I can't see him nearby, but I'm thankful the main doors are unlocked and the alarm is off.

From my pocket, I pull out the blu-tack I'd shoved in there before leaving the house. Breaking it off into small pieces, I roll it into balls and start putting the flyers up. Some I put on the lockers, some on the bare walls, and I even pin some on the noticeboard.

When I'm finished fifteen minutes later I stand by the double main door, admiring my handiwork. The flyers are of her sucking my dick. You can't see my face but Fallon is clearly in a compromising position. I've put her phone number and *'Call Fallon. She loves the D'* on it.

Loathing Temptation

I scoot out of the school building, going to get a coffee before I need to be back at school to watch the shit show.

Walking in half an hour later, I bump into Zeke at the front door.

I'm grinning like a damn lunatic.

He elbows me in the side, his other arm outstretched and his hand gripping the doorknob.

"What did you do?" he asks with a laugh.

"Wait and see," I reply winking at him before he yanks the door open.

The hallways are starting to fill and everyone is staring at the posters, gasping in shock, laughing. I'm only just inside the doors when I spot Fallon heading towards me. She's seething, steam practically coming out of her ears, but I can see even from a distance her cheeks are tear-stained and she's sobbing.

I can't help the laugh that escapes my mouth. I'm glued in my spot, watching as she has a meltdown—screaming—and ripping them off the lockers and walls. She scrunches them up into balls with her firsts, throwing them on the floor and stalking towards me.

"Woah, Fallon. Let up!"

"How could you Ashton?"

"How could I what? You think I did this?"

"I know you did! Those photos were supposed to be private."

I laugh at her, scoffing when I reply, "Oh Fal, you naïve bitch. You shouldn't let boys take pictures of you sucking their dicks now should you?"

"Well…you…you…" She cuts her words off, biting down on her lips and whimpering.

"What Fal? You wanna give everyone a show here? Show everyone how much you love sucking dick."

"No, I…I," she mumbles again, raising a hand towards my cheek.

My reflexes are too quick for her and I grip her wrist in my hand before her palm can slap against my cheek. I'm again about to hurl an insult at her when I hear the click clack of heels on the floor and Miss Masters' bellowing voice calling out down the hallway, "Fallon! Ashton! My office now!"

We both follow Principal Masters down the hallway to her office. I get a few high fives on the way, and Fallon looks at the floor the entire time.

Admittedly I feel a pang of guilt, remorse for hurting Fallon, but I had to do something to get the point into her head that she and I are done.

Miss Masters leads us into her office, ushering us both into a seat in front of her desk.

Miss Masters' office smells like sex and caramel from the oil burner she always has on, to mask the smell of her non-school activities. Word around the corridors is that Miss Masters is a bit of a hussy. I happen to know this for a fact, having caught Dad coming out of her office after school one day, adjusting his tie and the front of slacks; telltale signs of someone who has just been fucked.

"So, who is going to explain what's happened this morning?"

Loathing Temptation

I scoff under my breath. Fallon has turned mute, and is just glaring at me, and then to Miss Masters.

"Well, Fallon needed some payback served."

"You're admitting to putting up the posters, Ashton?" Miss Masters asks, stumbling on my name.

"Yes, Miss Masters. But punish me and I'll tell my Dad you gave me detention because I tried to get with you."

She lets out a whimper, and Fallon huffs, mumbling *seriously* under her breath before she stands up and rushes out of Miss Masters' office without a word.

"Fine. No detention, but every one of those posters will be taken down and the rest is to be thrown into the garbage. Anything like this again, and there will be harsher consequences Ashton."

"Like a spanking, Miss Masters?" I ask with a snigger. I'm sure my heinous father enjoys spanking her arse; the sick fucker.

Miss Masters blushes.

"Um. No. Of course not. That is not appropriate Ashton Castello." She practically purrs my last name, and it makes me want to chunder all over her desk.

Again I let out a sniggering laugh.

"Just teasing you, Miss Masters. It's a Castello men thing."

She doesn't entertain my taunt, only calmly says, "And you will apologise to Fallon."

I stand up, heading to the door.

"Yeah, sure," I mutter, leaving the office.

There is no chance in hell I'm apologising to Fallon. The entire school knows the details of our breakup thanks to her wayward mouth, and Beau sticking his nose in our damn business.

Kicking the papers still scattered around across the floor, I head to class, scooting in just as the bell rings.

Thankfully Fallon isn't in this class, but Tempany is and she won't stop staring at me. She thinks I'm a wanker.

Her sweet dark ocean eyes glaring at me give away all her emotions, and she's clearly turned on to. Glaring at her I lick my lips suggestively and make a wanking gesture with my hand and my tongue against my cheek.

She shifts in her seat—uncomfortably—and is most likely clenching her thighs together when she scoffs and turns away to look up the front at Ms Tate who's writing something on the board.

Tempany wants me, and fuck do I want her as well.

Even though she's the last girl I should want.

I loathe her, but I want her on her knees sucking my dick.

Fuck, I'm screwed.

Nineteen

Tempany

*S*ighing I kick the front door of the Castello's house—my new house—open.

I can't see where I'm going, lugging a big box of my books inside. I have no idea how I'm going to climb the stairs holding the box, without tripping. At the base of the stairs, I'm about to take a step up when I bump into something solid.

And it's not a something, but a someone. A guy, and he grabs the box from me, holding it against his chest.

"Hey, looks like you could use some help?" he asks, effortlessly walking backwards up the stairs, clutching the box to his chest still.

Caz May

I'm completely tongue tied, wondering who this gorgeous stranger in my new house is. I follow him up the stairs, fearful, but feeling comfortable enough to trust him.

He seems familiar and he's older for sure, maybe mid-twenties. He stops at the top of the staircase.

"I don't bite," he says to me with a cocky grin, that I've only seen one other guy exhibit. Ezekiel Alessio has the same signature smirk.

"I um...would you mind putting them in my room?

"Sure, show me the way," he says sweetly, his tone deep.

He follows me across the landing to my room. And I feel a little giddy when he steps into my space, putting the box down on the floor.

He runs a hand through his hair, flipping it back out of his eyes. I'm a dumbfounded idiot right now. And I'm trying to think back and remember who he is and if he's related to Zeke. I recall Zeke having an older brother, so I'm guessing this must be him, but I can't remember his name.

He breaks my thoughts from my trip down memory lane. "Don't remember me huh?"

I shake my head, smiling.

"Well, I'm guessing your Zeke's older brother?"

"Yeah, Dane," he says, stretching out a hand to me to shake. "And your Tempany yeah?"

Hesitantly I take his outstretched hand, his grip is firm and even though he's beyond gorgeous I don't feel any tingles or anything like when Ashton touches me.

"Yeah, how'd you know?" I ask nervously.

Loathing Temptation

"Ezekiel mentioned you were back. The way he went on about you coming back, I'm thinking my younger brother might have a thing for you."

I laugh, scoffing.

"Yeah, um. I don't think so. He um...kissed my best friend, Lorena."

Dane glares at me.

"Serious? You telling me, my moron of younger brother kissed the mayor's daughter?"

"Yeah," I reply with a snort of laughter.

"Damn, he's more of a moron than I thought he was. Speaking of him, you don't happen to know where he is?"

I nod.

"He skipped out with Ashton earlier. Obviously they didn't want to help my dad and I move in."

"Clearly," he replies scoffing and shaking his head. "Do you have anything else you need to bring in?"

I step out of my room, and he follows.

"No, I've bought everything in. Thanks for your help, Dane."

"No worries Tempany. I'll see you around. And if you see my brother around, let him know Mum's expecting him home early tonight."

"Oh ok, no problems," I promise, watching him walk out the door.

Closing it behind me, I head up to my room, collapsing on my unmade bed and text Lorena.

All moved in. Got some unexpected help

Ooo…spill girl?

Remember Dane?

As in Dane Alessio, Zeke's older brother?

Yep, that one. He's gorgeous.

Oh yeah. Anyway, dad wants something. I can hear him yelling. See you at school.

Putting my phone down beside me, I close my eyes. And feel my body drifting to sleep. I should put sheets on the bed, but that's too much effort.

I feel like I've run a marathon. I'm so exhausted, and this bed is so comfy, it is one of those memory foam ones that pull you in.

I imagine it's arms wrapping around me, making a mental note to ask dad about where my sheets are when he gets home, well, gets here from our old house. He'd been so busy getting everything sorted for moving into the Castello's that I've hardly seen him. And it's making me feel like an intruder in this house. It's certainly not a welcome to the household kinda day, considering everyone is out.

Despite what life was like with mum in Albury I want to go back there, at least I felt like I belonged there. Lockgrove Bay is just old memories and so far the new memories aren't pleasant.

I'm startled by my phone vibrating next to me. It's a text from an unknown number.

All sorted dear. On our way home with pizza.

Loathing Temptation

Ok.

I tuck my phone in my jeans pocket and head down the stairs. I'm shocked, nearly tripping up when Ashton comes crashing in.

"Temptress," he purrs, deliberately bumping into me at the foot of the stairs. His body pins me against the bannister. "Don't think you're welcome here, Tempany. This is my house. You're just standing in it."

I try to open my mouth, but nothing but a whimper comes out.

Ashton gets a kick out of my reaction, his chest rising.

"I'm guessing we're clear then," he practically seethes, shoving me aside and running up the stairs behind me.

I take in a deep breath to compose myself when my dad, Sascha and Ava come in—happily talking—with two boxes of pizza.

I honestly don't know what to do anymore, so I plaster a smile on my face, greeting them and following them into the lounge room to eat the pizza in front of the tv.

It's nice to have a proper family again, but my heart hurts because not everyone in this family is making me feel welcome.

Twenty

Ashton

The school year has barely started, and other than playing basketball, it's literal hell.

Tem and her dad have officially moved in, and I'm being expected to play happy families. Mum is expecting us—after eating pizza in the lounge room on Sunday—to now have dinner at the dining table, together. No phones, just eating allowed and small talk, which is admittedly torture.

Tempany stares at me across the table. I swear she deliberately sits across from me, just so she can stare at me.

Well, Temptress, two can play that game.

Loathing Temptation

I'm going to watch her like a damn eagle, tracking her—my prey—until I can find a time to strike and bring her down—to her knees—by crushing her sweet, I'm so innocent reputation.

I'd not had the chance to blackmail her, yet. Fallon had to be dealt with, and I'm not surprised she hasn't shown her face at school for like four days.

Parking the Camaro I head inside the school, wondering why everyone seems to be staring at me. It wasn't like this the other day when I put up the flyers. It makes me feel uneasy, and seeing Fallon standing against my locker when I walk into the school building makes me literally feel like chucking my guts.

Reaching her, I shove her aside.

"Care to move Fallon?" I taunt.

She whimpers and sniffs, making me realise she's sobbing. The girl is always fucking crying. And this time it's not of my doing, surely. She can't still be upset about the flyers. It's been a goddamn week.

"Ash, we, um…"

"What, Fallon? We what?" I seethe at her, slamming my locker shut.

"Can we talk in private?"

"Depends," I jeer, sniggering.

"Please Ash, don't be like that. I really need to talk to you, alone."

Tears are still stinging her eyes when she grabs my hand and pulls me away, towards the library. It feels like the entire school is glaring at me, and it's making my guts stir.

The library is quiet when we walk in, and she drags me into the shelves, away from any eyes on us.

"Well, talk Fallon," I taunt again, pushing her against the shelves. "Unless your tears were just a ruse to get me in here to suck my dick."

She scoffs at me, giving me dagger eyes. Ok point taken. Ashton Jnr is not getting a gobby right now. Good thing as he's not even half mast.

"No, we need to talk."

"Then talk, Fallon. I'm all ears. And we don't have until Christmas, so get on with it."

"I'm actually pregnant, Ashton. For real this time."

I actually laugh out loud, so loud I should be rolling on the floor.

"Oh right, sure, and it's mine."

"Yes, Ashton," she says softly. "I'm only a few weeks along. Maybe a month."

"I wore a fucking franger the last time we fucked, Fallon. And I'd bet you my Camaro the franger did not break."

"But the time before that, the week before remember?" She reminds me. And yes I fucking remember sticking my dick into her, bare when I went over to hers after fighting with Dad.

Still, it doesn't add up. I pulled out when I came.

"Well, even with that incident there's no way it's mine. I pulled out. And I'm not taking this bait, Fallon."

"I'm positive, Ash. I'm having your baby."

She's adamant, but I'm not falling for her bullshit.

"Yeah, Nah. Go fuck yourself, Fallon. Leave me the fuck alone, and for the love of all things holy, stop calling me Ash and thinking I give a shit about you."

I don't wait another moment to see or hear her reaction or reply before I'm racing out of the library. The bell sounding invades my headspace, and instead of heading to class I rush back to my locker, shoving my books inside and grabbing my phone to text Zeke.

Bro, skipping out this morning. You still got the jack and some grass around?

Yeah, meet you at the spot in ten

Sweet bro I'm fangin'

Ten minutes later, I'm leaning against the wall behind the gym when Zeke comes sauntering up to me with a bottle of Jack Daniels tucked under his arm. I practically snatch it when he hands it to me, opening it and taking in a few gulps.

"*Fuck,*" I mutter under my breath shaking my head, my hair flopping in front of my eyes a little.

"You ok, man?" Zeke asks, taking the bottle and leaning against the wall next to me whilst he takes a swig.

"Yeah, Nah, fuck!" I groan.

The Jack is good but hasn't taken away the uneasy feeling in my gut. If Fallon is really pregnant, I'm fucking screwed.

Fucked up the wazoo.

I turn to Zeke who's taking another swig and eyeing me questionably.

"You got that grass, man?"

"Yeah," he replies, reaching into his pocket for the joint and a lighter. He hands them to me, and I take a long drag after lighting it, puffing the smoke out after holding it in my head a moment.

"You gonna tell me why you were fangin' so bad? We haven't smoked in yonks."

I take another quick drag, heading it and handing Zeke the half spent joint. He takes a quick drag.

"Ash, man," he says softly.

"Um yeah, Fallon might be knocked up for real."

Zeke nods, but his eyes show the fear I'm sure is reflected in mine.

"Yours?"

"Yeah," I mutter worriedly, my words hitting me in the guts.

"You always wrapped ya dick though," Zeke retorts.

I shake my head, grabbing the Jack Daniels from him for another swig.

"That's not true. I fucked her bare the week before we broke up."

"Shit man. That's fucked up. What ya gonna do?"

"No idea. Avoid her, and hope it sorts itself out."

"Yeah, anyway bro, I'm gonna sneak this back into my locker before the bell. You coming back to class?"

"Yeah, the grass is hitting me, but I can't afford to skip the whole day. Dad would be on my arse if he found out I wagged the whole day."

"Sucks man, sucks," he replies as I follow him inside, making sure the corridor is still empty before we head to our lockers.

Zeke shoves the Jack Daniels in the far corner of his locker, grabs out his books and slams it shut.

Loathing Temptation

"Catch ya at lunch," he tells me, walking off when the bell rings.

"Not recess?" I yell to his back.

He turns back, making a thrusting gesture with his hips.

"Got a date in that place, if you get my drift," he hollers, sticking his tongue out.

I flip him off.

"Oh Ezekiel, I get your drift you sicko."

I quickly grab my books out of my locker and head to class.

The hit is getting to me, and I'm regretting my choice to get high at school.

I could so go for a nap right about now.

Twenty-One

Ashton

Somehow I manage to get through until last period, without falling asleep. But in the last class, History I give in to the overwhelming tiredness plaguing me from my high comedown.

I'm startled awake by the class laughing around me.

Mr Smith's history class is never funny so something else must be making everyone cack themselves.

Sitting up I glance around the room, noticing that everyone is staring at me, and pointing whilst doubling over in laughter.

In front of me, Fallon is sitting in a chair, her legs crossed. And she's twirling a sharpie between her fingers.

I feel Tem step up behind me. She leans down to my ear, exhaling a breath that sends a jolt through me.

"She wrote something on your forehead," Tem whispers in my ear. I jump up from my seat, rushing out the door to the bathroom.

And looking in the mirror, right across my forehead in capital letters is the word, 'ARSEHOLE'.

The bell sounds, and I quickly rush out to the Camaro before anyone else sees me. I notice Tempany rushing out to her car as I drive off, and honestly, I just want to get home and get Fallon's scathing word off my damn head. It makes me feel sick to the stomach, because I don't want to be that guy.

Fidel Castello is an arsehole.

And I don't want to be.

Fifteen minutes later, I'm home and rush into the bathroom. Grabbing a face washer I run it under warm water, squeezing a bit of liquid soap onto it as well.

Looking in the mirror, I start scrubbing at my forehead, but the black sharpie word of shame won't budge. I let out a silent scream, and turn to the open bathroom door to find my stepsister standing against the door frame, taunting me.

"What do you fucking want?" I ask angrily, glaring at her a moment before resuming my scrubbing.

"You won't get it off like that...with that," she offers, stepping into the bathroom.

"Did I ask for your help, Tempany?"

She makes me seethe with her response. "Do you want it off or not?"

"What the fuck do you think?"

She bites her lip, stepping around me and our eyes lock on each other's in the mirror.

"It's kinda true," she tells me, opening the drawer full of makeup.

"Yeah, rub it in, Tempany," I reply bluntly.

In her hand she's gripping a makeup remover wipe.

"May I?" She asks.

I don't reply, but sit on the toilet lid and she moves to stand in front of me. My whole body is suddenly on fire, her crotch practically at my face, and I can smell her arousal and her peachy body wash.

"It might be a little cold," she tells me pressing the makeup wipe to my forehead.

With one stroke she wipes it across my skin, and it leaves my skin feeling all tingly. That's not the only place I'm feeling tingly, my whole body is erupting in goosebumps. And she's not even touching me. Why I'm having any kinda reaction like that to Tem being close to me is crazy. But fuck.

"Is it coming off?" I ask with a sigh.

"Yes, arsehole," she taunts with a smirk.

"Funny Temptress," I taunt back when she wipes my forehead again, stepping back. I miss having her so close straight away. And that's so bad, so fucking bad.

"Done, you're not branded an arsehole now."

"Thanks, I guess," I mutter softly.

"You're welcome, Ash," she tells me, dropping the wipe in the bin, and walking out.

Loathing Temptation

My nickname on her lips sounded so sweet, and standing up I look in the mirror again wondering if she really sees beyond my 'arsehole' exterior.

Heading out of the bathroom, walking past Tem's room her door is ajar. Peeking through the gap I can see she's getting changed, slipping her skirt down over her pert arse exposing her toned legs.

Leaning against the wall, I peek in to watch her, loving every second of her exposing more of her sexy body to my eyes.

I can't help myself, my hand slipping down to the front of my daks. My dick is throbbing, and I palm it, touching myself over my trackies. Biting my lip, I hold in the moan that wants to escape my mouth. I'm so turned on right now, and she's not even touching me. This is so fucking bad.

I'm tempted to whip my aching dick out—standing in the middle of the hallway—when Tem turns around, her eyes nearly catching mine.

Groaning, I rush into my room, flopping down on my back to the bed. My dick is tenting my trackies, aching so bad for release.

I don't have this kinda reaction to a half naked chick; ever. And I shouldn't be having such a reaction to Tem, my fucking stepsister. But fuck.

She's sexy as fuck, and that's mainly because she has no idea that she's a walking wet dream.

Yanking my dick out of my trackies—thanking myself for going commando—I start to jerk off, stroking my dick in long strokes, closing my eyes and imagining Tem's hands on me. I'm so hard, so close to blowing my load all over my t-shirt.

Caz May

Sitting up a little I lift the white t-shirt I'm wearing over my head and throwing it aside I'm shocked to find Tempany has come into my room—even though my door was closed—and she's standing in the middle of my bedroom with a shocked expression painting her pretty face. She takes a tentative step towards the bed, her eyes gazing over my nakedness. If my daks weren't around my knees I'd get up and push her down to her knees to suck me off. But I'm practically pinned to the bed with her stare. And to tease me more, she bites down on her lip, letting a moan slip through.

She's about to turn away, so I grab her hand—pulling her down onto the bed—not letting her leave without some payback for coming into my room without knocking.

Her whole body is stiff, but through her T-shirt, I can see her nipples hardening. She still can't take her stormy eyes off of my dick.

"You gonna help me, Temptress?" I taunt, smirking at her, and squeezing her hand still gripping mine.

"Um. No. I. Um. Can't," she stammers, shifting a little on the bed.

I'm fucking loving that I'm clearly getting to her, and just watching her reactions is making my dick throb more.

God, I want her hands on me, her mouth taking my dick in to choke on it.

Trying to get up her other hand brushes against my thigh, and she flinches a little accidentally touching the tip of my dick.

Fuck, even that is good.

Her eyes lock on mine, and she whimpers, her chest moving as she takes in a breath, and brushes her fingers along my length.

My dick feels like it's on fire, and I want to explode. Ash Jnr is going to combust if her hand doesn't stop the sweet torture. I grab her hand, stopping her from touching me—even though her touch is absolute bliss—and I flash her a teasing smirk.

"Temptress you've seen me, it's only fair you show me your pussy," I taunt, my hand reaching under the tiny skirt she's wearing. I swear to god, she has no idea that the clothes she wears practically scream I'm a sex kitten, I dare you to touch me.

She shifts a little again, biting down on her lip and again letting out a sexy moan when I run a finger over her pussy, teasing her through her knickers. They're so wet, showing me my Temptress is turned on.

I need to see her sweet pussy up close.

"Stand up Temptress," I demand.

She doesn't say anything and doesn't stand.

"Oh really, you gonna disobey me huh?" I taunt, grabbing the elastic of her knickers and yanking them off her. The fabric rips surprisingly easily and the force brings her body closer to mine.

I scrunch up the knickers in a fist, sniffing them. And fuck me dead, I'm gonna crave the sweet smell of her pussy. And fuck do I want to taste her.

I lift up her skirt to look at her pussy, and groan taking in the glorious sight. I didn't expect her pussy to be anything but a full bush, so I'm shocked and excited to find a neat landing strip of hair. I can see her arousal, and I'm so tempted to slide a finger inside her. She's looking at me with anticipation—and I want to savour that look—have her begging me to touch her, and taste her.

Without warning, I push her away, and she stands up from my bed. I follow, pulling up my daks awkwardly. I mentally tell Ash Jnr I'll attend to him later; whilst sniffing Tem's knickers.

I give her a smirk as she walks out, tucking her knickers in my pocket and I tug my t-shirt back on quickly so I can watch her arse as we head downstairs for dinner. It takes a helluva lot of self-restraint to not reach out and touch her arse, touch her pussy, knowing she's commando in the shortest skirt known to man.

At the dining table, we sit down next to each other. I look across at Ava sitting across from me, and she's smiling like she knows something I don't.

"Lovely, now we're all here, Matias will you lead us in grace?" Mum says, softly, giving Tem's dad a sweet smile.

This happy family thing is bullshit. I don't want to act like I want to welcome Tempany and her dad into our lives. He's obviously putting on an act for my mum, drawing him in by being Mr nice guy. But he left Tempany all those years ago, and her being here with him and acting like she actually loves him all seems like lies to me. Lies like Tempany not remembering taking my basketball. There's only one other liar I hate more and that's Fidel Castello, and we all know what a pathological liar and arsehole of epic proportions my daddy (not so) dearest is.

Matias starts speaking, "Tonight we join hands."

I take Tem's hand, leaving it resting on her thigh under the table. Her skin warms at my touch, and her breath hitches, her stormy eyes warning me before closing them as her dad continues, "And we thank our dear Lord for bringing us together as a family, and for this food we are about to enjoy. Amen."

Loathing Temptation

My eyes lock on Ava's, and we both nod and repeat 'Amen', not with our usual chant. She huffs like she's annoyed at me, but I frankly don't give a shit.

We start eating and Tempany yanks her hand from mine, staring at me as she starts to eat, but I don't move my hand from her thigh. Instead, I edge it higher, slipping it between her legs, almost brushing my fingers against her pussy. Mum eyes me with a smile.

"What were you two doing upstairs together?" She asks with concern in her tone.

I take a bite of my steak, gulping it down hard with the lump in my throat.

"Just studying," I reply, teasing Tem with a stroke of my finger against her wet pussy. "Tem was helping me study biology."

"Oh, that's great, son. I'm glad you're getting along and helping each other."

"Yeah," I reply to Mum, removing my fingers from Tem's pussy. She actually whimpers, and mum gives her a questioning look, before looking to her dad and nodding at him.

"Tempany, honey, are you ok?" he asks with that bellowing fatherly voice.

"Um, no, I'm not feeling well. Can I be excused?"

"Of course, dear. I'll come and check on you later," Mum replies, too sweet and caring for my liking.

I glare at mum.

"I'm sure Tempany will be fine mum. I'll check on her after dinner."

"Oh thank you, son, that would be lovely."

Tem stands up, smoothing her skirt down, to obviously not show her pussy to us all. Not that I'd mind seeing it again, and fingering her properly.

She walks out, turning back to look at me. I smirk and wink at her, my back turned so our parents don't see me put my finger into my mouth.

And holy fuck.

Tasting Tem's arousal on my finger makes my dick instantly harden.

Only the fact that I'm still sitting at the dinner table is stopping me from racing up to Tempany's room to make her feel better with my fingers and tongue buried in her pussy.

I've never had this reaction to just one taste of any girl. And I'm shit scared about what that means. Tempany is getting to me. Why can't I just hate her? Why do I have to want her in all sorts of dirty ways?

Loathing Temptation

Twenty-Two

Tempany

*W*alking into Target, I feel a little overwhelmed by the winter clothes that have started to take over the shelves, even though it's not even autumn yet.

Flicking through the pretty long sleeved skater style dresses for my size, I'm taken aback when Lorena suddenly blurts out a question. "How it is living with your hot as hell nearly stepbrother?"

I grab the dress in my size, admiring the dusty pink fabric dotted with flowers.

"Um, it's fine," I mutter, biting down on my lip and heading towards the underwear section. I need some new knickers and

Caz May

bra's but I have a feeling Lorena is going to make me buy the most unpractical underwear, just because.

I pick up a lacy bra, putting it back before Lorena sees it.

"He um…" I mutter, cutting my words off, and grabbing a cute lacy knicker and bra set.

"He what girl? Spill!" Lorena screeches at the top of her lungs, so loud, I swear everyone in the entire store is now glaring at us.

I grab her arm, yanking her away towards the change rooms.

"I can't tell you here."

Again Lorena's voice is way too loud for being in the middle of Target. "Ooo, did you fuck him? And finally lose ya v-card?"

"No, um," I mutter, kicking myself for my lack of words as we sneak into the same change room at the very back.

Lorena sits on the stool, an eager smile on her face. I hang the dress and underwear up. I'm not planning on trying them on, sure they'll fit me. I look to Lorena then, who's checking herself out in the mirror. She doesn't turn her head back to me when she says, "Tell me Te."

I feel giddy that she called me Te. And I honestly can't believe I'm about to say the words that spill out of my mouth, "I um touched his dick."

Lorena stands up, her mouth agape for a moment.

"Ooo," she coos excitedly. "So you gave him a handy?"

She's so excited I feel silly for clearly being a disappointment and to innocent for my own good.

"Well, no, he um didn't you know," I tell her, my cheeks aflame when I continue, "But I kinda showed him my vagina to."

Lorena laughs, playfully smacking my arm.

Loathing Temptation

"Ooo, dirty girl. And it's a pussy or snatch. Or anything other than a vagina, Te."

I blush even more. "Um, I can't believe I just told you that."

Lorena laughs again, before asking, "So have you kissed him yet?"

"No, I shouldn't have done anything," I snap, a little angrier than I intended. "He's my stepbrother, Lo."

She shakes her head and I wonder for a moment if she wants Ashton, even though she's told me she's not into him.

"So? You want him don't you?"

I bite down on my lip, muttering through my pursed lips, "Well yeah. But he hates me."

"Whatever, Te. He wants you. And you want him. Just go for it." Her words are demanding and I feel like I'm being told what to do. I can't deny that the thought of kissing Ashton—and touching him again—excites me a lot more than it should. I'm getting that all to familiar tingly feeling, and my stomach is full of butterflies thinking about Ashton touching me.

"Yeah um...I." I cut my words off, unsure of what to say, or what I should be confessing to my best friend.

"And wear this..." Lorena says, breaking my thoughts and holding up the lacy knicker and bra set. I blush.

"Um if you say so," I reply, turning the handle to head out of the change room.

"Oh, I do," Lorena says with a laugh following me out.

We laugh together as we walk out to the registers and I decide to ask, "How're things with Zeke?"

"Oh um yeah," Lorena says a little ashamed, her head low, looking down at the floor. "We've fucked a couple of times. But he's not exactly the boyfriend type."

I can tell her confession hurts. That she doesn't want the words she's saying to be true.

"Yeah, maybe you should tell him that you like him?" I suggest with a smile, whilst elbowing her in the side.

She looks up, smiling and replies with a laugh, "Buy these sexy knickers to promise you'll seduce Ashton and I'll think about it."

"Fine, but I'm not making any promises like that. I just happen to like these."

"Whatever you say bestie," she jeers at me.

After paying for my items we leave together, and my mind wanders to thinking about sleeping with Ashton, what it would be like to actually lose my virginity, and I don't know whether losing it to Ashton is a good idea. He's going to break me regardless, and one touch from him makes me feel like dropping dead.

Anything else, and I'll turn to ashes at his hands.

Twenty-Three

Ashton

Every month I dread this day. And tell myself I'm a coward—every time—for even still entertaining his bullshit.

I'm eighteen and I'm still acting like a child who has to do everything daddy tells me. I should just tell him where to go, to fuck himself up the arse, but the beating I'd endure after telling my father that would be agony, and worse than the agony of heading to the Castello castle. I still laugh at that—the name his house has around town—but it's kinda true.

Dad's house is huge—especially for one person residing there—and it has turrets and about five balconies. I don't remember much from when we lived there, having moved into the other house when Ava was two. Why Dad never sold it is beyond me and watching it come into view again at the end of the most prestigious street in Lockgrove Bay my stomach twists, and I feel like I'm going to chunder all over the inside of the Camaro—which would be mega shit—because I just got it detailed recently after Ava spilt her ice cream everywhere after our beach day out.

The cast iron gates of dad's castle open as I drive up to them, so it's clear he's expecting my arrival and that makes my stomach twist even more.

These monthly check-ins are hell, and today I'm even more anxious because I need to put my little sister in the firing line to see if our dad actually has a heart.

Parking the Camaro out the front, I cut the engine, getting out to find Dad standing on the porch with a whiskey in hand. He doesn't say anything when I step up onto the porch, just nods at me as I follow him inside to the parlour.

Yes, his 'castle' has a fucking parlour.

He gulps down his whiskey, offering me one, which I decline, knowing he'll not actually give it to me if I say yes anyway.

"So, son, things seem good with your grades so far?" he says as a question like he doesn't know the answer.

"Yeah, I'm doing fine. Maths is fine if that's what you're asking."

"Good, keep it that way. And study extra hard for your exams. No basketball."

I scoff. "Yeah, sure dad."

He's staring at me like he's telepathically trying to will me to do what he wants. Sorry daddy, not going to happen.

Loathing Temptation

"So is there anything else you need to tell me? How's Ava?" he asks pretentiously. He doesn't give a shit about his daughter. And that's confirmed by my next question. "Are you planning to do anything with Ava for her birthday?"

He chuckles, a deep evil chuckle that makes my blood boil with anger.

"I'm giving her a fucking car Ashton. Isn't that enough?"

"Right. So you're not even going to see your own daughter for her sixteenth birthday?"

"No!" he seethes, slamming his whiskey glass down on the bar top. "If she wants to see me, she knows where I live."

I know I shouldn't say the next words, but they fall out of my mouth before I can stop them, "Come on dad. Don't be an arse."

His anger boils over, and he's stalking towards me, balled fists. "What'd you say to me boy?" he spits at me, his rage clear.

"You heard me," I snap back, berating him with my tone.

I shouldn't poke the bear, but he makes me so fucking furious.

"Oh I heard you Ashton Oliver, and how dare you!" he snarls at me.

He's in my face, right in front of me. And he unclenches his fist, his arm raising up to my cheek in slow motion. I feel the contact of his open palm against my cheek when he slaps me, but the room feels silent.

It's wrong, but I poke the bear again, taunting him with threats. "Go on dad. Hit me again. Mum knows what you do to me. And I'll tell Matias Davies too.

"Oh no, you didn't just threaten me, boy," he taunts me, chuckling maniacally when he continues, "Matias fucking Davies doesn't scare me. Your pathetic excuse for a mother can have him."

His words stab at my heart. They fucking hurt. His utter disdain for my mother, who he supposedly loved.

"Pathetic huh?" I taunt, stepping back a little. "At least he doesn't beat his own flesh and blood."

"You have no idea child," he sneers at me, again with the chuckle. I'm a little taken aback by those words, wondering what he knows about Tempany's dad. I know there's some secret he's hiding, lies that are hiding under the lovely caring dad persona he's putting on whilst slipping into my family. I'm not having it and I'm not spending another minute with my own arsehole of a father either.

I turn to walk out the door—without another word—but dad pulls me back, his grip so hard on my arm I screech in pain from the Chinese burn his fingers give.

My head cracks back to glare at him, to beg him to stop and his stare is cold, evil and callous.

"You need to watch ya mouth son, or you can kiss the house, your car and your trust fund goodbye," he bellows at me, his grip on my arm harder with each threatening word.

"Yeah," I snigger. "Bite me, dad. And fuck you!" I roar, spitting in his face as I yank my arm away, anger flaring.

I back away towards the door, giving dad an up yours and go fuck yourself gesture before walking out. I get straight into the Camaro and gun it out the open front gate. I shouldn't have done that, because Fidel Castello's fury has no limit. And his threats are real. That I can be certain of.

Twenty-Four

Ashton

The change rooms are empty when I slip out of the showers after practice.

Zeke the dirty coward had pissed off home to shower in serenity as he put it. He only heads home to shower if he's desperate for a wank, and honestly, right now I can't blame him for that.

I've been thinking about Tempany way too much, and Ash Jnr gets way too excited when thoughts of kissing and touching my stepsister spring to mind. I'm telling myself it's because he hasn't gotten any action—other than with my hand—since Fallon and I broke up two months ago, but it's not that.

It's my temptress.

Caz May

She'd get any guy rock hard—without any idea—just from a look. And that's without even a glimpse of her sexy as fuck body, her wide fuckable hips and tiny waist. Her body is made for sin, and I know I shouldn't want to but I want to take Tempany to church, to worship her body and then confess all the dirty things I want to do to her.

Once out of the shower, I go to grab my towel from the hook behind me, but it's gone.

Fuck, great.

I quickly run around the change rooms, but there's no towel in sight. They've all been taken for washing. Clutching my dick, I awkwardly hobble out into the locker area, glancing around to make sure no one is around.

I'm nearly at my locker when I hear a giggle and feet scuffing on the tiled floor.

I brush it off, but I'm furious when I find my clothes aren't where I left them on the bench seat by my locker. The only thing next to my bag are my black Adidas sneakers and a note.

Ashton,

I took your clothes.

So good luck getting home without everyone seeing how tiny your dick is.

And goodbye.

The note is clearly from Fallon and honestly makes no damn sense. I'm kinda worried I'm holding some fucked up suicide note

Loathing Temptation

in my palm, and I scrunch it up angrily. I hate Fallon, but I don't want her dead. I don't want that shit on my conscience, especially if she's actually knocked up and is about to off herself and my unborn child.

I slip on my sneakers, standing up from the bench seat after and slinging my bag over my shoulder. I use it to cover my dick, with my hand holding it in place as I head out into the corridor. There are still a few students around, and hobbling out of the change rooms like I'm trying to hold a shit in my arse I head down the corridor as fast as I can. The jeers and laughter of my classmates follow me, and I'm nearly at the double doors to run out to my car, barearsed and free when I bump into someone.

"Oh Ashton, I'm sorry," the voice says, stopping me in my tracks when I realise it's Principal Masters.

I gulp, trying to slip past her without saying anything. But she grabs my arm, pulling me forcefully towards her office. I'm trying not to panic. I'm fucking naked and my dirty daddy fucking principal is taking me into her sex dungeon.

Ok her office but still, I'm naked.

She slams the door behind us, stalking around to sit in the chair behind her desk. I sit in the tub chair in front of her desk, strategically making sure my bag is over my junk.

Ms Masters is tapping her manicured nail on her desk and biting her lip. It's creeping me the fuck out because I feel like I'm about to be taken advantage of.

Fucking Fallon for putting me in this situation.

Ms Masters is probably excited that's she's about to fuck another Castello man, and I'm about to chunder.

Maybe this is some fucked up dream, and I'm not really in the principal's office naked and about to be violated.

I grab the skin of my wrist, pinching it and flinch, an *'ouch'* escaping my lips.

I need to get out of here now, but I don't want to give Ms Masters the satisfaction of seeing my arse as I head out the door.

Motherfucking shit, I'm so fucked.

"Ms Masters, am I in trouble?"

"No, Ashton. You're not in trouble," she says with a laugh that rubs me the wrong way.

No Ashton, fuck, that's all kinds of dirty and wrong. Miss Masters is not going to rub you, any way.

"So can I go? And make a run for my car?"

"I can't let you go outside without your clothes, Ashton."

"Well, I didn't plan on streaking. So if I'm not in trouble, and you promise not to look at my arse, I'll be going." I stand up from the chair, still holding my bag in place so her eyes that rake over my body don't get a view of my dick.

"Ashton, please just wait a minute, and put these on," she says, handing me a pair of trackies and a matching hoodie.

She's fucking glaring at me when I take them, and I turn around so she at least only sees my arse. I hope she closes her damn eyes, but who fucking knows.

I drop my bag, and slip the trackies on, and then tug my arms into the hoodie sleeves, rolling them up to my elbows before I turn around and pick up my bag to head out.

"Thanks, Ms Masters. I'll return them next week."

"No need Ashton, they're spares. Keep them."

"Um, ok, thanks, I guess."

Loathing Temptation

Again I turn to the door to leave, my hand on the doorknob when she says, "Ashton please, sit down again. We need to have a chat."

Great, she's going to punish me after all, and I'm going to get a beating from dad for being a fuck up when it wasn't even my damn fault.

"I thought I wasn't in trouble?"

"You're not, but we still need to talk."

I sit back down, my heart hammering in my chest.

I honestly don't know what to say, or do, or think.

I can't stop clenching my fists.

"Fallon came to see me before I bumped into you in the hallway."

"Oh," I mutter, anger bubbling as it's obvious she took my clothes to get back at me.

"She told me that due to the incident that happened a few weeks ago, she has decided to leave school."

"Oh, shit, really? I apologised. I shouldn't have done that, but Fallon is a daft bitch and she wouldn't rack off."

"That's not appropriate language to use in here Ashton, despite the circumstances."

"I'm sorry," I mutter under my breath.

"I'm guessing she took your clothes, to get back at you?"

"Yeah, I'm guessing so," I mumble.

"Well, I'm sorry about that. I'm not going to punish you for streaking, Ashton. And no I won't mention anything to your father."

"Thank you, Ms Masters. I appreciate that."

Again, I stand up.

"I really need to be getting home. We've got some things being delivered for Ava's birthday party tomorrow."

"No problems Ashton," she tells me, coming back around to the front of the desk, smoothing down her pencil skirt.

I give her a smile and she returns it.

I open the door, heading out and she quickly says, "Your arse is sexy. I won't tell your daddy I checked it out."

I don't dare turn back around to see the look on her face.

My whore of a principal—who fucks my dad—just confessed that she checked out my arse.

I'm gonna chunder. And I'm going to get her dirty arse fired and bring my vile father down with her.

Loathing Temptation

Twenty-Five

Ashton

Ava's party is in full swing, her friends and some of our younger cousins are all crowded in our rumpus room, dancing and drinking. A few of them seem like they're tanked, but I don't really care. Mum gave me permission to have a couple drinks myself, with the promise that I wouldn't let anyone underage drink on my watch. And I haven't. Not my problem if someone else has bought alcohol.

I spot Ava's best friend—Dakota Neelson—chatting to some of their other friends loudly over the music on the other side of the room. But my sister is nowhere to be found.

I head over to Dakota, and she smiles at me when I approach, reaching out to give me a hug. She's always been like another little sister to me, which is why I don't honestly need another one.

Caz May

"Hey Ashy," she taunts me.

"Hey Kota, have you seen the birthday girl around?"

Dakota blushes, gulping like she's hiding something from me. "She, um, went upstairs for something. I can go find her if you want?"

"Nah, all good," I reply, walking away with my mind racing. Because not only is my sister missing but so is my best mate. The only reason I agreed, and let Ava even invite him is that he's practically family. He might spit out the sexual innuendo about Ava, but he's my best mate, my brother from another mother.

I put my drink down, and head upstairs, instinctively. Ava's door is ajar, and I can hear her giggling. And the whispering voice of my best mate, *'Av's, shh.'*

My sister replies, *'Make me, Ezekiel.'* And I practically hit the roof, tiptoeing across the landing to her room. Stepping into my sister's room I find my best mate and sister wrapped around each other, against the wall. His lips on hers. He's fucking kissing her. My best mate is playing tonsil hockey with my innocent little sister.

The anger is coursing through me like a freight train. They're so lost in each other they don't even realise I'm in the room. And I'm both furious and utterly disgusted by what I'm witnessing.

I want to lay into him so hard.

Clearing my throat I wait for them to realise my presence in the room. Zeke's back is to me, and he turns, horror on his face at what I've caught him doing. He mutters a breathy, *'Fuck'* stepping back and I yank him away from Ava, yelling, "Fuck you! You fucking bastard! How dare you kiss my sister!"

Loathing Temptation

He has the gall to chuckle before replying calmly, "Well, I couldn't let her be sweet sixteen and never been kissed."

"You didn't just say that Ezekiel," I jeer, rolling up my sleeves and balling my fists. I barely think about my actions, even with his cocky grin still on his mug when my clenched fist pummels into his jaw.

"Fuck, Ashton!" he bellows, his hand cupping his jaw.

I'm still fuming, and Zeke isn't moving, but about to put up a fight against me. I catch him off guard, another punch hitting his nose, another his eye. I step back, glancing at my little sister who's sobbing next to me.

"Why Ashy? I...I asked him to."

"Doesn't mean 'he' should've, Ava."

Zeke is darting his gaze between us, trying not to wince from the pain I've inflicted. Blood is dripping down towards his lips, and I lift my fists up again to taunt him.

"Fuck you with a ten foot pole up the arse, Ashton. You're a fucking tosser," he seethes at me, before turning his attention to Ava for a moment.

"Av's, I'm going to go. Happy birthday, gorgeous."

"Thanks, Ezekiel," she purrs at him with a sweet smile as he walks out.

Ava clutches the teddy bear in her hands tighter against her chest.

"I hate you, Ashton. You ruined my birthday."

"No, Ava. He ruined your birthday. And I'm not going to forgive him for this."

She sniffs back tears.

"No, if you need to be angry at anyone, be angry at me. Not Ezekiel."

"Ava, he kissed you. Even after I told him to stay away from you. He broke my trust."

"You told him to stay away from me?" she asks through sobs.

"Yes. He's not the guy for you, sis."

"I'll make that decision," she says defiantly, heading out of her bedroom in a huff, still clutching the teddy bear.

I feel like the worst brother in the world. And now I've also most likely lost my best mate; fifteen years of friendship obliterated with my fists.

The party is still going on downstairs, but I don't care.

Care factor zero.

I'm an arsehole.

An arsehole who is turning into the one person I hate the most; Fidel Castello.

Like father, like son as the saying goes.

I head out of Ava's room to my own and flop down on my bed. And I don't stop the tears that spill from my eyes.

Loathing Temptation

Twenty-Six

Tempany

I t's been an odd week since Ava's birthday party. The tension in the air in the Castello household is so thick. I don't know what happened at Ava's birthday, because I skipped out and stayed at Lorena's for the night, not wanting to intrude on her party when I barely know her.

I feel like an intruder now too, stepping into the bridal boutique with Ava and Ashton's mum to get the bridesmaids dress and wedding dress.

Being included in the wedding planning makes me feel special, and like I'm being welcomed into the family, even if that isn't the case. Ashton has barely spoken to me, or to anyone since the birthday party. At the dinner table, he just eats and grunts annoyance if anyone tries to speak to him. I'd tried to talk to him —actually knocking on his bedroom door—but he's just ignored me. It's not making being in the Castello household very homely and welcoming.

In the bridal boutique, Ava and I sit down on the couch in the middle of the dressing room, whilst we wait for her mum—my step mum—to come out and show us her wedding dress.

Ava is scrolling through her phone, a scowl on her face. I can't stand the tension anymore so I ask softly, "Ava, did I do something wrong?"

She looks up from her phone, and smiles, laughing softly.

"No, why would you think that?"

"You haven't spoken to me since before your birthday. I'm sorry if my not being there upset you."

She sniffs like she's trying to hold back a sob.

"No, it's not that. Something um...happened."

"What? You can tell me."

"I know," she says softly, scooting closer to me on the couch and smiling. "Ezekiel kissed me."

"Oh wow!" I blurt out, shocked.

Ava blushes and smiles wide.

"Definitely wow. It was amazing."

"Yeah," I muse softly, and she continues with giddiness in her voice. "It was the most amazing first kiss ever, and he gave me a teddy bear. I think I'm in love with him."

"That's great Ava, but why have you been so down this week then? Did he force you to go further?"

Loathing Temptation

"No nothing like that. But Ashton caught us and hit him. It was horrible. My brother told his best friend to stay away from me."

"Oh, that's intense," I tell her, nodding.

Her words confirm why the tension in the Castello household has been on edge all week.

"Well, you'll see Zeke at the wedding. Maybe you can tell him how you feel? I'm sure Ashton will come around if he knows how you feel."

"Yeah, that's if he's still at the wedding. Ashton said some really hurtful things. This is the first week I can remember that they've not spoken to each other. And I feel kinda guilty about it."

I'm about to reply when my step mum comes out of the change room in a strapless cream mermaid gown. She looks absolutely stunning.

"Wow, mum, you look beautiful," Ava says beaming, and standing up to hug her mum.

"Thanks, honey. I feel beautiful in this dress." Her eyes lock on me, still sitting on the couch. "Te, do you think your dad will love it?"

I stand up, tentatively walking towards her, unsure of how to approach this moment that seems really intimate.

"He'll love it, Ms Castello," I tell her with a smile.

"Please, Te, I told you to call me Sascha. And come here for a hug."

I step closer and she wraps Ava and I into her arms, kissing our hair. I sniff back the tears stinging my eyes. My mother was never like this, and Sascha barely knows me, and is acting more like a mother to me than my own did in my entire life.

"So, mum, what colour are our dresses?" Ava asks with a wink directed at me.

I'm dumbfounded and look between them both when I ask, "Our dresses?"

Sascha smiles, laughing softly.

"Yes, your dresses. Tempany, I'd love for you to be my maid of honour."

I'm shocked, giddy. And did I say shocked?

"Oh my gosh? Really?"

"Yes, dear. It would mean the world to your dad and me to have you be such a special part of our day. What'd you say?"

"I'd love to, mum," I reply, wondering for a moment if I should've let that word slip out. But her smile tells me that it was welcome.

"Fabulous, you'll both look amazing in the navy blue dresses I've picked out," she says eagerly when a sales assistant comes over holding two dresses that are stunning. They're short, with thin spaghetti straps and a V-neck line in a soft billowy navy blue chiffon.

"Oh my, mum, they're amazing," Ava announces squealing.

"Yeah, I love it. I can't wait to wear it," I say with a smile. "I think we might need to wear a nude strapless bodysuit under them."

The sales assistant smiles, and then says softly, "Yes, you're right and we have just the thing. I'll grab one for both you and we can finalise it all at the register once you're changed, Sascha."

Sascha nods at her, shuffling back to the change room.

Whilst we wait I smile at Ava, but she doesn't return the smile. And that has me a little worried.

Loathing Temptation

"Ava, are you upset that your mum asked me to be maid of honour?"

"No, Ashton is the best man, and you're older than me. Makes sense. And I'm still in the wedding party."

Now, I'm even more worried. My stepbrother is the best man. Of course, it makes sense, but he'd be better off partnered with his sister.

"Who's the other groomsman?" I ask hesitantly.

"Ezekiel," she announces, a smile curving her lips.

"Oh, well that explains why you're happy then," I reply with a laugh.

"Yep," she says, laughing as we follow her mum out to pay for all of our dresses.

We're each handed a suit bag with our dress and bodysuit inside. And heading out to the car, I can't help but smile.

Maybe things are going to get better. Ashton might still hate me, but the rest of his family seems to be welcoming me with open arms and that makes me feel happier than I've been in forever; since I left Lockgrove Bay ten years ago.

Twenty-Seven
Tempany

Once back home, I take my dress and bodysuit into the bathroom to try them on. I've barely put on the bodysuit when the door opens, and Ashton walks in. He eyes me, licking his lips and I swear I blush from head to toe. This bodysuit is nude lace, and most definitely see-through.

Ashton's eyes darken looking at me and instinctively I raise my hands to cover my boobs. But that doesn't cover the rest of my exposed skin, my crotch is also exposed to his lingering gaze.

I find my voice, screeching, "Ashton seriously, get out! Don't you know how to knock?"

He shrugs, not caring at all that one, he's barged into the bathroom unannounced and two, that I'm in revealing underwear. His gaze roams over my body, and I feel completely exposed, as though I don't even have the lace covering my body.

He lets out a moan, again licking his lips. His eyes are full of lust, and I shiver, my skin erupting in goosebumps. I'm scared of what he's going to do, but I'm also turned on and giddy.

"Damn, temptress, that bodysuit is sexy as fuck," he taunts, his gaze again taking me in from head to toe. He drops to his knees in front of me, and I stifle the squeal of triumph I want to let out when his hands grip my thighs, prying my legs open.

"Ashton, what the hell?" I scream out, before covering my mouth with the back of my hand. I don't want anyone else to know he's in the bathroom with me. He shouldn't be in the bathroom with me.

*And oh holy what the, oh my dear god, he's...he's...*He's licking up my thighs, his tongue tasting the smooth flesh, and he's murmuring softly like he's loving every second.

"Ashton, stop, please," I beg, feeling as though my knees are about to buckle.

He stops, looking up at me with a cocky smirk.

"You really want me to stop?" he asks, reaching between my legs, and running a finger along my crotch.

Oh god, that feels good. So good.

I shake my head. I've never felt this way before, and seeing Ashton on his knees for me is strangely thrilling. Before I can think or utter a word, he stretches up towards my crotch, his head between my legs and he licks me through the lace.

A rush, a shiver of pleasure courses through me, and I stumble a little, letting out an *'oh'*.

Ashton stands up suddenly, not saying a word and walks straight out. I shake my head, wondering if I just imagined him being in the room. But the fact I'm turned on—more than I ever have been—it's clear I didn't imagine my stepbrother practically going down on me.

Only one other thought is tumbling in my mind, and that's why the fuck hasn't he kissed me. I never curse, even in my head.

But Ashton gorgeous as fuck Castello—yes as fuck—makes me want to scream out *'fuck'* and all manner of naughty words repeatedly whilst he does bad, bad things to me.

Oh, god help me.

I'm falling for my *'fucking'* stepbrother.

Twenty-Eight

Ashton

L eaving Tempany in the bathroom after licking her delectable pussy through the lace of the sexy as sin bodysuit she was wearing, Ash Jnr is screaming for release in my daks. One taste of my temptress had me craving more, and the second taste literally brought me to my knees.

I'm so fucked. And I so want to fuck my temptress, hard until she's screaming my name.

With a raging hard on I stumble to my bedroom, dropping down on my bed and yanking my daks down to my knees.

Slowly I start to stroke my dick, rubbing my hand up and down my length. Thoughts of my temptress sucking me, fucking me and riding me fill my head and my breathing has turned to pants.

Caz May

I've never been this hard from any sexual encounter. I honestly don't think I ever fucked Fallon with Ash Jnr this hard. And I'm angry at myself for letting Tempany get to me. Angry at myself for giving into how she's making me feel.

I'm blaming my fucked up emotions right now. The fact that Zeke has tried to apologise to me with countless texts, that I've not answered. I'm the worst best mate on the planet for what I did. And I'm shocked that he still wants to speak to me. He broke my trust and it hurts worse than a mega case of blue balls, but fuck I miss him.

I'm still stroking my dick, trying to not let thoughts of my best mate fill my head because as much as I love him—and miss him—I'm not going there.

I'm so pent up from thinking about Tempany, my dick throbs in my hand and I come all over my t-shirt, the very minute my phone starts vibrating on my bedside table.

Glancing at it I see Zeke's name and picture flashing on my screen. There's no time like the present.

Sitting up I grab my phone and answer, "Speak Ezekiel."

I decide taunting him is the only way I'm going to not be a pansy and cry, or scream at him for being a tosser and making moves on my little sister.

"Hey, dipshit. Nice of you to finally speak to me."

"You're lucky I love you like a damn brother. Doesn't mean I'm going to forgive you."

"Point taken. And I'm sorry, Ash man. I fucking am, but Av's...fuck she can kiss."

I pretend to vomit.

Loathing Temptation

"I don't need to hear that about my little sister. And even so, you won't be kissing her again," I tell him authoritatively.

He sniggers under his breath, and I take a deep breath in to not give him a tongue lashing down the phone. If he was here, I'd have to rein in my anger to not lay into him again with my fists.

"Right, well that's not why I called," he starts, taking in a deep breath.

"So you just called to say you missed me, then?" I jeer, laughing.

"Who'd miss you," he taunts back, clearly rhetorically. "I was just wondering if you wanted to meet up to play some ball."

I nod, even though he can't see my response.

"Yeah, ripper man. Need to get out of the house."

"Ripper, Beachview Park in fifteen?"

"On my way. Catch ya," I reply hanging up and sighing.

Beachview Park. The basketball court where my temptress bought me to my knees.

Just what I fucking need.

Standing up I quickly strip from my t-shirt, wiping it across my stomach to collect the remnants of my come. I pull on my blue basketball guernsey and plunge my trackies to the floor, before tugging on my basketball shorts. I don't put any boxers on. Going commando under my basketball shorts always feels better.

Grabbing my keys and my phone, I head out to the Camaro, concentrating on breathing. I think about shooting Zeke a text to head to the other basketball court, but Beachview Park is closer to his house, and considering he's walking I decide against it.

When I get to the basketball court—Zeke is already there—dribbling and bouncing a brand new basketball around the court. Stepping up to him I steal it away, blocking him and making an easy shot. The ball sinks straight through the net, and Zeke intercepts it, dribbling it back towards me.

Again I nab it from him, and he stumbles, falling against me. Instead of grabbing the ball, his fingers grip the waistband of my shorts and stepping backwards he daks me. My shorts fall to the ground, and Zeke shrieks in horror.

"Dude eww, heard of jocks man?" He asks, mocking me as I tug my shorts back up.

"Fuck you, man," I roar back, giving him the finger.

"Nah, but seriously dude. Why you hanging loose?"

He punches me playfully in the arm. And I can't believe I'm about to admit what I was doing when he called. But he'd have been doing the same, most likely thinking about my sister. I shake that uncomfortable thought away and reply, "When you called I'd just finished wanking, if you must know."

He chuckles.

"Oh right. Thinking of Tem?"

I feel myself blushing. I'm going to give myself away and he'll be grilling me.

"No, that hot model, Barbara Palvin," I tell him with a nod to try and convince him.

As always my best mate can see right through my bullshit, and calls me out, "You liar man. You don't even think she's hot. You were so jacking off thinking of Tem."

Loathing Temptation

Fuck, why does he have to know me so well?

Might as well admit it.

"Fine you know me too well bro," I admit, biting down on my lip a moment before continuing when Zeke nods.

"But fuck me, I walked in on her in the bathroom, and she was wearing sexy lacy see-through underwear, a bodysuit."

Zeke's eyes light up, and I honestly don't want to know what's going through his dirty mind. I have some idea that it's most likely something to do with my sister. And if I'm going to keep my temper in check I can't think about that.

"Nice man...tell me you smacked one on her?" He asks, giving me a suggestive wink.

Dirty tosser.

I shake my head, thoughts of my tongue making contact with Tem's pussy through the lace filling my head. Ash Jnr stirs in my shorts.

Fuck. Fuckity. Fuck.

"Nah, man. I licked her pussy through the lace and fuck..."

Zeke's eyes boggle at me.

"Damn man. You dirty boy," he jeers at me, rocking his hips in a sexual gesture. "You need to fuck her into next week."

"I know," I reply with a nod. "But I can't."

"Suit yourself," he says oddly before adding with a smirk, "maybe I'll go after her, since Ava is off limits."

That makes the anger bubble in my guts.

"You wouldn't dare fucker," I roar at him, lunging at him with my fist balled.

His hands go up in surrender after he shoves them into my chest to push me away and calm me down.

"Chill dude. I'm not gonna steal ya chick," he promises, still with the smirk. "But grow some balls and take her. Or someone else will."

I mumble *'better not be you'* under my breath, before grabbing the basketball by Zeke's feet to continue playing our game of one on one. I hit the ball to bounce it hard in an effort to try and curb my anger. I need to stop letting it get the better of me, or I'm going to end up like him.

And that makes my gut twist.

I will not be Fidel Castello and I'll stop thinking about Tem.

Yeah, scratch that last part—because I'm so thinking about the next thing to ruin my stepsister.

My temptress is going to have her innocent act ripped away, along with that lace bodysuit. Ash Jnr is already screaming in my shorts just thinking about it.

Fuck Tempany Davies, fuck her hard.

Twenty-Nine

Tempany

I t's crazy how quick the first few months of the year have gone, and it's even crazier that I'm at the rehearsal dinner for my dad's wedding to Sascha tomorrow. I'd chosen a really pretty, very low cut dress in white chiffon. It swishes as I walk, and I feel really giddy in it.

The giddy feeling could also be because the whole night I've been staring at Ashton and I'm practically drooling. He's wearing dark grey slacks, and a baby blue button down shirt with the sleeves rolled up to his elbows. He looks good enough to eat, and all I'm thinking about even during the speeches after dinner is kissing him.

Caz May

Since the licking encounter, I've thought of nothing else. I want him, even though wanting my stepbrother is so wrong. No boy has ever gotten to me the way he does. Never made me feel the way he does.

After the speeches, I'm scanning the room and see Ashton slip away, sneakily. He's heading towards the hallway at the back of the venue. I follow him after a few minutes, not really sure why I'm even contemplating such a crazy idea.

But I kinda want to get him back for the bathroom licking me incident.

When I first walk down the hallway, he's nowhere to be found. I shrug, turning to head back to the table for the after dinner refreshments when I feel his presence behind me.

He's coming out of the bathroom. My eyes take him in, and I stop him a moment stepping into his personal space. He doesn't move.

So, I invade his personal space more, backing him against the wall.

"You ok, temptress?" he asks with his sexy smirk.

"No, I have to tell you something," I tell him with a smile.

"Like what?"

Again I move closer to him—our bodies pressed against each other—before whispering in his ear, "I think about you touching me."

I reach down between us, cupping his dick in my hand. He's turned on—at least I think he is.

He lets out a moan, and huskily teases, "Oh really temptress, you want me to touch you right here, right now? This dress you have on is so damn sexy."

I don't dare reply to his question—yet.

Having this control over him is oddly thrilling and the fact that we could get caught in the middle of the hallway is affecting my body too.

It's really dirty.

"No...but..." I stammer, letting out a moan myself, feeling his dick getting harder in my grip.

"But what temptress?" he taunts, with that wicked smirk again. It makes my knees feel weak.

I don't reply.

Ashton is trying to hold in his moans, but the throaty sounds he's making are loud and when I fumble with the button of his slacks he doesn't even flinch.

Not even when I slide the zip down and dak him, pushing his grey slacks down over his arse. He's wearing tight white boxers, and his dick is straining against them.

"Fuck temptress," he murmurs, when I slip my hand inside the boxers, teasing him by rubbing my hand all over his dick.

"God, Tem, don't stop. Fuck."

I let out a giggle, pulling my hand out of his slacks and stepping back. I stare at him for a moment before walking off, leaving him standing against the wall with his dick hard and his pants around his feet.

Take that stepbrother.

Caz May

Thirty

Ashton

I'm at a wedding, my mother's wedding, standing next to my new stepdad. And it feels fucking weird. Yeah, I want my mum to be happy. But why she has to be with Tem's dad, of all people on the fucking planet is beyond me.

At the altar I'm standing next to Matias who is fidgeting like he's a nervous wreck. I could be the good stepson and reassure him, but I don't really give a shit about his feelings. I'm here, standing up at the altar next to him, for my mum.

Zeke is standing next to me as the other groomsman. His eyes practically fell out of his head when Mum asked him to be in her wedding. But it makes sense. He's practically another son, since he's at our house probably more than his own half the time.

Loathing Temptation

Mum clearly has no idea that he made moves on Ava. I should've said something, but Mum was so happy to have him be a part of her special day and honestly having him standing up at the altar with me is the only thing that's making being a part of this wedding bearable.

If we hadn't made up on the basketball court—after I beat him to nearly a pulp last week—then I'd probably still be a crying mess at home in bed.

Zeke's my brother, no matter what. But my little sister will always come first. And speaking of the brat, she's started the walk down the aisle, as the music for the bridesmaids' entrance has started. It's some instrumental, classical crap and torture for my ears. I glance at Zeke next to me, slapping him on the arm because his eyes are nearly falling out of his head watching Ava walking towards us.

"Don't even think about it dickwad," I warn, nodding towards my sister.

He licks his lips, grunting before replying, "But Fuck man. She looks sexy as fuck."

"Seriously man, can you not?"

"What? She's probably wearing a lacy g under her dress."

I elbow him again.

"Ow, and don't tell me you aren't about to cream ya daks thinking about Tem in that dress."

Again I don't voice a reply. Of course, I'm thinking about Tem's sexy lace bodysuit. Thoughts are racing through my mind of getting another look at it later when we're home alone. I give my best mate a wink and laugh, taunting him, "Get ya mind out of the gutter."

"It's already way past the gutter. I'm totally stripping Ava in my head," he jeers, giving her a wink as she steps up to the altar to stand on the opposite side.

"And stop thinking about my sister like that arsehole," I tell him.

He chuckles, grating on my nerves.

"Um yeah ok," he replies, adjusting his dick in his slacks. I snigger at my best mates misfortune.

But it's then that I'm in the same boat myself, with Ash Jnr deciding to say hello in the front my daks the moment I see Tempany coming down the aisle. She looks every bit the temptress, the dress dipping to show just a hint of cleavage and her hair around her shoulders in soft waves. I'm thinking of slipping the straps down her shoulders, and watching the dress fall to the floor when Zeke whispers to me, "You should have fucked her when you had the chance."

"Yeah," I murmur, licking my lips and winking at Tem when she steps up to the altar and stands next to Ava.

She nods towards the aisle where my mum has now started walking in. She looks absolutely beautiful.

And so incredibly happy.

Reaching the altar, she gives me a quick kiss on the cheek, and then Ava as well, before Matias steps forward and takes her hands with his.

The pastor starts the ceremony then—and I tune out from the words—glaring at Tempany from across the aisle.

It's totally wrong, now she's officially my stepsister but I still want her sexy body as mine.

I still want to ruin her.

Thirty-One

Ashton

After the ceremony and all the formalities of dinner and speeches, I'm being dragged onto the dance floor by mum. "Dance with Te please dear," she says softly in my ear. I grunt my annoyance, before heading back to the bridal table, and grabbing Tem's hand.

"We've been summoned for a dance," I tell her. She smiles at me, and it makes my stomach flip.

Fuck me. Why is she fucking getting to me?

She follows me onto the dance floor, that's now full of dancing couples. When I put my arm around her waist to pull her closer she murmurs which makes Ash Jnr jolt in my slacks.

I need to think of dead rodents. I'm going to have a hard on if I have to dance with Tem any longer.

Her arms around me, and her body pressed against mine as we move slowly across the dance floor is like sweet torture.

I can't help but think of her naked in my arms, our bodies rocking together in dirty ways.

No, Ashton, stop. Dead rodents, Dead rodents. Fuck!

I need to step away from Tempany now. I'm seriously going to cream my black slacks. Thankfully the music stops, and the next song is more upbeat. Tempany steps back, retracting her arms from around my waist.

"Thanks for the dance, Ashton," she says softly, with that smile again.

"Um, yeah, no worries, Temptress," I reply with a smirk, turning away to head to the bathroom to deal with Ash Jnr.

Once I've dealt with Ash Jnr in the bathroom, getting him to calm himself down with a splash of water on my face, and a little stroke in the toilet stall I head back out to the reception.

Even over the music blaring out from the main room I can hear the unmistakable giggles of my little sister.

That would be fine if I didn't also hear my best mate's chuckle and the sound of their lips locking together.

Rage takes over my body and I search them out, finding them in the alcove leading out to the balcony.

Zeke's jacket is open, his shirt untucked, with my little sister's hands all over him. Her dress is practically around her waist, and her leg is wrapped around his thigh.

They're locked at the lips and practically dry humping each other. I'm completely flabbergasted that I'm catching them out kissing again; this time in public.

Stomping towards them, I grab the back of Zeke's jacket, yanking him away from my sister. He yelps in pain and turns to me. I look to my sister for a moment, and she's giving me dagger eyes, begging me to not hurt him this time. But I'm livid.

Without warning I lay into him, pushing him down into the ground and pummelling his chest with my fists.

"Ash, man, stop!" he yells at me, spit hitting my face.

"I told you to leave her alone, Ezekiel!" I bellow at him.

"I couldn't...I...I...want her," he says softly, biting down on his lips as though he's not saying the words he really wants to.

I don't have anything to say this time, and I raise my fist to hit him in the cheek when I feel hands grabbing my jacket.

"Ashton stop you're hurting him," a voice behind me says meekly when hands that seem small—but are strong—are pulling me off even when I still want to pummel my best mate.

Standing up I find that Tempany has pulled me up. She's still clutching my jacket when she drags me out to the balcony.

My breathing is ragged, harsh and the anger is still raging inside me. Again I'm angry at myself for acting like dad. Again I used my fists, letting the anger get the better of me.

Tem pushes me against the wall and looks at me sweetly.

Her eyes are dark, and I'm drawn into them. I look down to her lips a moment, but barely have time to form another thought before she's stretching up on her tiptoes to kiss me.

Caz May

It's a sweet soft kiss, barely a brush of her lips against mine, but it ignites something inside me.

And I want more.

I snake an arm around her body, not letting her break the kiss, but pulling her closer.

Deepening the kiss, I take her mouth with mine harder, licking her lips for entrance. She lets me in with a moan.

And I'm about to explode.

This kiss.

This kiss is everything.

Everything and more.

I've seriously waited my whole life for a kiss like this.

An intoxicating, pull me under type of kiss.

Her lips feel beyond incredible on mine, and breathless I pull back.

"Fuck temptress," I curse, giving her a smirk.

I want to kiss her again when she doesn't reply, but she takes her hand, smiling at me.

We walk back into the reception together to watch our parents leaving.

Everyone—including my traitorous best mate—is forming an arch for our parents to run through. Tempany and I join the end, on either side, next to Ava and Zeke. I give him a death stare, and he nods across at Tem.

Fuck it. I can't stay mad at him, after that kiss with Tem, I'm on a high.

Before my mum reaches us, I whisper in Zeke's ear. "I kissed her, and fuck…"

Loathing Temptation

"That good huh?"

"Better," I tell him when mum reaches us.

She gives Ava and I a hug, before taking her new husband's hand and heading out the door.

I can't stop smiling. Partly because my mum is happy again, but also because I can still feel Tem's kiss on my lips, and I want more. Fuck her being my stepsister.

My little sister is about to walk away, thankfully not with Zeke and I stop her a moment.

"Av's are you still staying at Kota's?"

"Yes, is that ok?"

"Yeah, great. I'll see you tomorrow."

She heads out, and I head back to the bridal table to pick up my stuff. Tem is there, and she's smiling like the cat that got the cream.

I feel the exact same way, and when we get home I'm tasting some cream.

Thirty-Two

Ashton

Tempany slides into the Camaro, with her bouquet on her lap. It pushes the dress down between her thighs, and Ash Jnr is loving that. My mind is racing with thoughts of what I want to do to her when we get home.

Driving is incredibly difficult with my temptress sitting next to me in her dress, whilst imagining taking it off her and having my wicked way. Ash Jnr is throbbing, and thankfully the drive home is short—partly because I gunned it like a madman—and the Camaro purred for me.

The moment we head inside I want to kiss her before we're even up the stairs. No one—but for us—is home, so I could take her anywhere I want but I'll at least let her get to her bedroom. It's closer than mine.

I follow her into her room. She's gazing at me warily. And I stalk towards her until her knees hit her bed. She bites down on her lip, and I groan, the desire to kiss her again coursing through me. She's going to kill me. My temptress is going to take me to heaven, or hell because I'm about to go down in flames.

"Why'd you kiss me Tem?" I ask, seductively.

She gives me a shy smile.

"To calm you down," she says softly, again biting her lip.

That little gesture has never been a turn on for me, but when my temptress does it, *fuck, fuck and oh fuck.*

"Oh yeah?" I taunt, rocking my hips against hers so she can feel my dick hardening. "Well, it didn't work."

She cocks her head to the side.

"Huh? I don't get you," she replies meekly.

"You, my temptress have not calmed me down. Quite the opposite," I tell her, winking and giving her a dirty smirk before I lick my lips.

She lets out a sexy whimper.

"Oh, I'm sorry..." she says, clearly not sorry at all.

"Did you love it, temptress? Love having my tongue down your throat? Fucking your mouth."

She blushes but doesn't reply, just stares at me. Her eyes are dark, hooded with lust. And I don't doubt that her pussy is as wet as fuck and throbbing.

"Temptress?" I say her name as a question, needing a reply to my question. She didn't push me away. And she kissed me first.

So I'm not doubting she loved it as much as I did.

"I...I loved it," she stammers, her tone husky. And fuck does that declaration turn me on even more.

Ash Jnr is so rock hard now.

Harder than ever.

Tempany Davies is going to kill me.

"Loved what temptress?" I taunt, loving that my questions are getting to her from her little whimpers.

Again she lets out the sexy little whimper, moan sound and replies, "You kissing me. And..."

"And what?" I taunt, running a hand up the side of her thigh, slipping it under the dress. "You want more?"

I squeeze her thigh, and she moans again, softly replying with her eyes locked on mine, "Yes...yes Ashton...kiss me again."

I chuckle.

"You sure Temptress? Do you know what happens when you play with fire?" I taunt her, squeezing her thigh harder, loving how her skin heats with my touch.

She nods.

"You burn to ashes, Ashton." My name on her lips is the best sound I've ever heard.

This time I moan—not able to stand the tension between us for a second longer—kissing her hard. This kiss is even more arousing and intense than the first one. Her lips on mine, her tongue lacing with mine is literal heaven on earth.

I could die right now. And my only regret would be not fucking her.

God, I want to fuck her, so hard.

Loathing Temptation

Breaking the kiss, I'm practically breathless, panting out my words, "Fuck, you can kiss Temptress."

"Um, really? You like kissing me?" she asks innocently.

"I fucking love kissing you, temptress."

"Oh, um," she mutters, blushing a deep crimson.

Her innocence turns me on, bad.

"And I don't want to just kiss your lips," I tell her, my eyes on hers, my hand grazing the edge of the lacy bodysuit, right at her pussy.

"Oh, um...what?" she mutters again.

Yanking the buttons open, not caring if I break them I run a finger along her slit.

And holy fucking shit! Her pussy is so wet.

"Mmm, so wet for me, Temptress," I tease with a groan.

She shuts her eyes for a moment when I slide a finger inside her aroused body.

"Oh, um...sh...it..." she stammers, biting down on her lip again.

"Open your eyes, Tempany. Look at me."

She obeys, and Ash Jnr loves that, throbbing in my slacks.

Her eyes flutter open, taking me in with lust flaring in them.

"Take off your dress," I demand, taking a step back from her for a moment.

She doesn't say a word, just continues to stare at me whilst she slips the straps down her arms.

The dress falls to the floor, and she's about to do the same with the bodysuit, and whilst I'd love to see her naked it's kinda turning me on more to see her hard nipples through the lace.

I shake my head.

"Leave that on," I demand again. "And lie down on the bed, spread your legs for me, Temptress."

She follows the instruction, her eyes never leaving mine, even when I kneel on the bed at her feet, yanking her legs apart more so her pussy is exposed to me.

Slowly, with my eyes locked on hers, I insert a finger into her wet pussy. She bucks her hips up.

"Eager huh, temptress?" I taunt, pushing another finger inside when I feel the resistance of her innocence against my first finger. She lets out a pained whimper when I push through.

"Ok temptress?" I ask, feeling a little guilty for taking away her innocence this way. But at least if I get to fuck her, I can go hard, slamming my dick into like I desperately want to.

She whimpers again, and then softly says, "I'm ok."

"Want more?" I ask, my fingers pressing up to hit her g spot, again making her hips buck and this time a pleasurable moan escapes her lips.

"Oh, sh...it...yes, yes, Ashton."

I take my fingers in and out, fucking her with them and her moans are so illicit. They're making Ash Jnr throb in my slacks. And I know Tem is close to coming, so there's only one thing to do.

The thing I've been craving for weeks since I first saw her in this bodysuit.

I lean down, pressing a kiss to her clit. She almost screams out her pleasure. And I fucking love it.

Taunting her and teasing I still my fingers inside her, pressing her g spot again, and biting down on her clit.

Her pussy pulses around my fingers and she comes for me, letting go in a sudden convulsion.

Loathing Temptation

I withdraw my fingers, looking down at them to see the spots of blood. Not giving a shit I wipe my hand over my slacks and lean over her to kiss her. She grabs my cheeks, pulling me closer as she devours my mouth, teasing me with moans against my lips, tasting her arousal on them.

When she breaks the kiss she's breathless and pants out her words, "That. Was. Incredible."

"Oh, you bet it was Temptress. Wait till I fuck you. I'm going to make you come so hard, you'll see stars."

She bites down on her lips and mutters through her teeth, "That was my first...um...orgasm."

I chuckle, leaning closer to her again to teasingly whisper, "First of many, temptress."

She gasps and gives me a quick kiss which I break.

"But first you need to return the favour," I tell her, nodding towards my aching dick.

"How? You want me to touch you?"

"No, temptress. I want you to suck my dick."

"Oh, I've never...I...I don't know...how to," she tells me stammering and sitting up on the bed a little.

I stand up, undoing my belt and yanking my slacks down to my ankles. I kick them off, and pull Tempany off the bed, pushing her down to her knees.

"Fuck, you look sexy on your knees, temptress," I taunt, pulling my dick out of my boxers and stroking it a little.

"Suck it, temptress," I command.

She whimpers and nods, reaching up to grab my length in her fist. Her fingers on my skin feel fucking incredible, sending shivers rushing through my entire body.

I'm so fucked.

Tem then looks up at me, her tongue darting out from between her lips to tentatively lick the tip of my dick. Precum is already seeping out, and she laps it up, licking her lips after.

I'm ready to come apart from just that teasing, and that never happens. I need a good, hard sucking to get off, but with Tempany just having her touching me has me so on edge.

Still, I taunt her, "Temptress, you need to put it in your mouth. Dicks don't suck themselves."

She giggles, and without warning, she takes my dick into her open mouth, between her pink lips.

And oh holy fuck!

Her mouth on me. Her fucking mouth on me, her tongue swirling over my tip, over my length as she takes me in and out of her mouth. Absolute fucking ecstasy.

Nothing—other than fucking her—is ever going to feel this good. She takes my dick out of her mouth for a moment, taking in a big gasp of air, innocently asking, "Was that good?"

"Fucking fantastic, temptress. Can you take more?"

"More?" she asks, gasping.

"Take my dick all the way, temptress. Deep down your throat." I lift her chin, grazing a finger down her throat and my dick once again disappears between her lips.

Grabbing a fistful of her hair, I push her down onto my dick and push it deep down her throat.

And holy shit...fuck...fuck!

I'm going to come so hard. She gags on my dick, and pulls back a little, not withdrawing all the way.

Loathing Temptation

"Fuck Tem, I'm going to come," I tell her, yanking her away by the hair, and fisting my dick with my other hand.

My come spurts out in ropes, spilling all over the front of her bodysuit. I don't say anything, don't help her up before tucking my dick back in my boxers and walking out of her room, leaving her kneeling on the floor by her bed.

No doubt she's confused. But my head is a spin. I've never come so hard and my dick is still aching.

I need more from Tempany. But I know I shouldn't want anything with her.

I'm an arsehole, who just took my stepsister's virginity by finger fucking her.

An arsehole who made a virgin suck my dick. And the worst thing is, I'd do it all again, and then some.

I want to—need to—fuck my stepsister.

Thirty-Three

Ashton

Even though I just came all over Tem's lacy bodysuit my dick is still aching for release. I'm blaming my thoughts of wanting to fuck her. I want to walk back into her room and pin her down on the bed. I want to kiss her all over and slam my dick into her pussy.

Anyone would think I'm whipped. But I'm not going there. I'm not falling in love again, ever.

I'd loved Fallon. Well, I thought I'd loved her, but she'd never made me feel this way. So completely mesmerised from just a couple of kisses, and a damn good gobby.

Fallon never made my dick ache, even after release. And never made me instantly hard just thinking of her, or with a simple touch.

I need to let go. I need to get my temptress out of my head.

Instead of heading to bed, I go into the bathroom. I'm angry with myself for giving into Tempany. Angry at myself for being such an arsehole, but seeing her pleasure written all over her face, fuck it wrecks me.

I'm wrecked.

Tempany is my fucking stepsister. I can't have her. But I want her.

Fuck, fuck, FUCK!

Stripping off the rest of my suit I throw it on the floor. Turning on the water, I don't even let it warm up before getting in the shower. It's cold, but I'm still thinking of Tem—and how she'd look naked—so my dick is still hard as steel, and the cold water isn't having the desired effect.

Leaning against the shower wall, I jerk off, stroking my dick and trying not to let out moans. I'm not soon going to forget how her lips felt around my dick, how she took me deep and the forced gag she made when I hit the back of her throat.

Fallon could suck a dick hard, but she could never deep throat. I hardly ever got off from her sucking me. And with Tempany.

God, help me, I'm screwed. So screwed.

I need to stay away from my stepsister. I need to go back to bullying her, to take back the control and take my balls back.

Right now I can feel them pulsing, a release building in them and with one final stroke of my dick I come, ropes of cum shooting out across the tiles whilst I'm screaming out *'Tempany'*.

I'm hoping she didn't hear. But then again, maybe it would be good if she did.

No, no. Bad idea.

Cleaning up quickly, I turn off the taps and get out of the shower, wrapping a towel around my waist and I head to my bedroom.

Dropping the towel to the floor, I pull back my sheets and slide under the covers, naked.

For a moment I think about going into Tempany's room and making her mine completely. But I know that's a really bad idea. She's my stepsister. And wanting my stepsister this much is wrong. Plus I loathe her. I loathe Tempany, but fuck, I want her.

I close my eyes, reliving the night in my head. I can still feel her kiss on my lips, and her mouth on my dick. And drifting to sleep, despite it being wrong I think about the next time I'll get to be with my temptress.

Thirty-Four

Tempany

*L*orena is sitting on my bed, clutching a bowl of popcorn that she's shovelling into her mouth. She's eating like she's starving, as not only is she shovelling the popcorn in but she's already had two slices of the Hawaiian pizza sitting on my bed. I take a slice, taking a bite so I don't have to talk to my best friend. She's glaring at me, concern all over her face because I'm extra quiet tonight.

"What's up? You've been acting weird since the wedding," she declares, before shovelling more popcorn into her mouth.

"Nothing. Just Ashton being annoying," I tell her, putting my half-eaten slice of pizza down in my lap.

"Yeah? How so?"

Caz May

"Glaring at me. Brushing past me. And being really mean again," I confess, thoughts of Ashton making me feel all tingly again.

"Is that all? I feel like you're holding out on me, Te."

I take a big bite of pizza, gulping it down before blurting out, "He kissed me. And he…"

Lorena playfully pokes me in the stomach.

"What? Tell me you fucked him?"

"No, but he touched me, and licked me until I had an orgasm," I tell her and she smiles so wide I think her face is going to crack. "And I…um…sucked his dick."

Lorena spits out her bite of food.

"You what?"

"You heard me, Lo."

"Did he come in your mouth?"

I shake my head. "No, thank god."

I can feel a blush rising up my cheeks. "But I can't stop thinking about it, Lo."

"Yeah, I bet," she says a little down.

"Like honestly, all I'm thinking about is kissing him, and everything. I don't know what to do."

"Well, I say go for it. You know all the way. He clearly wants you."

I shake my head at my best friend. She's clearly lost the plot, forgetting that despite what has happened between Ashton and I, he's off limits.

"He's my stepbrother Lo. My dad would hit the roof if he found out I have feelings for Ashton."

She laughs, slapping my thigh. "Who said anything about feelings?"

I feel a blush rise up my cheeks, not believing myself that I'm about to admit to my bestie that I have feelings I shouldn't for my bully of a stepbrother.

"Me, Lo," I start, feeling a weird weight lift off my shoulders, admitting it out loud. "My feelings for Ashton are so not brotherly."

She's glaring at me, and I don't know what else to say, or what she's thinking. I continue, "But for some reason he hates me."

She shakes her head at me this time, then nods like she's as confused as I am.

"Yeah I don't know. But theres a fine line between love and hate Te."

My best friend is right. That saying rings true with Ashton and me, at least in my case. I'm positive that Ashton hates me. All he wants to do is to taunt me, and force any sexual advance on me he can. I shouldn't want that. That should make my gut turn, considering my past experiences, but with Ashton it makes me all tingly, and I can't help but give into the temptation he taunts me with.

A smile curves my lips, and I reply to Lorena, "Yeah true and temptation is hard to fight."

"Exactly," Lorena says with a laugh. "Maybe just sleep with him. And see how you feel then."

I contemplate her words, about to reply when she says, "Lose ya v card properly and then move on."

"So use Ashton to take my virginity completely?" I question her.

"Exactly," she says with a nod.

Again I think about it for a moment. And just the thought of having sex with him is getting me excited, thinking back to our first kisses, and the way he touched me and licked me, until I let go.

"Maybe," I surmise, biting down on my lip whilst I think for a moment. "But I have no idea how to get him to sleep with me. He kinda left me hanging the first time."

Lorena laughs, her head tipping back when she suggests, "Put on some of that sexy lingerie and go into his damn room."

"Yeah," I muse yawning. "I'm beat."

"Me to," Lorena replies, pushing the pizza box to the floor whilst I pull back the covers, climbing into bed.

Lorena climbs in next to me and we lay on our backs, looking up at the ceiling. I flick off the bedside lamp and the glow in the dark stars on my ceiling glitter.

I smile in the darkness, asking Lorena, "Lo, when did you lose yours?"

I hear my best friend gulp, and take in a deep breath before she replies, "Um...to Jonathan Rea after my sixteenth birthday. I got really drunk."

"Oh, you never told me that," I comment, a little shocked.

"Yeah, I wish I could take it back," she tells me, her voice pained.

"Yeah, why's that?"

"I should have saved it," she grumbles. "But then I wouldn't have wanted to be a virgin with Zeke."

I can't help the giggle that escapes my lips. We've both got it bad for the Lockgrove Bay Preparatory kings.

"Oh you really like him, huh?"

Loathing Temptation

I feel her shake her head in the darkness next to me, the pillow shifting with the movement.

"I don't know. He's gorgeous, and the sex is amazing. But I don't think he wants a girlfriend."

My heart breaks for my best friend. Ezekiel is an arsehole and I hate that he's making my best friend feel this way.

"Maybe you should tell him how you feel," I suggest.

"Yeah, when you tell Ashton," she teases back with a laugh.

I laugh with her, our giggles filling the air.

"Not happening," I say, closing my eyes.

"Whatever you say, Te. Let's get some sleep."

"Yeah, goodnight, Lo."

"Goodnight, Te," she replies, letting out a yawn.

I sigh, and let my mind drift to my stepbrother. I want him, but it's wrong.

Thirty-Five

Ashton

Another Monday of monotony at school is drawing to a close with P.E class.

Miss Miller again has us lined up on the basketball court, with skipping ropes. Why she has to inflict this stupid torture on us is beyond me. I'm eyeing Tempany standing across from me, watching her netball skirt flipping up at the front whilst she jumps the rope.

I stick out my tongue, making a suggestive licking gesture to her when her eyes lock on mine. She practically falls over her own feet, and I laugh, puckering my lips to blow a suggestive kiss to her. She gulps. And licks her lips, looking down at the ground before starting to skip again.

Zeke elbows me in the side. "You fucking her with that stare bro?"

Chuckling I reply, "Nah, riling her up. Gets me hard watching her blush." I nod towards my shorts, where Ash Jnr is threatening to have a party.

Dead rodents, dead rodents, I repeat telling him to calm the fuck down.

"Damn man, you're whipped," Zeke teases me. He's always fucking dogging me, and I can't help biting back.

"Am not. She's my stepsister," I reason, trying to sound convincing.

Zeke chuckles. A deep belly laugh that makes me want to punch the smirk right off his mug.

"Right, so you're not wanking thinking about her every night? Wishing you could fuck her mouth, and then take her tight virgin pussy as yours?"

"No," I snap. *Yes, fuck yes.*

"Right, pull my dick dipshit. You're whipped for your stepsister, and you need to nail her. And move on."

Move on. Yeah, fucking right.

"I don't want to hurt her," I muse, frowning and giving my best mate *'go fuck yourself arsehole'* eyes.

He gulps, shocked by my statement as much as I am. "Seriously? What happened to hating her with a fiery passion?"

I bite back, "Didn't say I don't still hate her."

"Yeah, you did. When she first moved back you hated her so much you wanted to ruin her," he informs me like I've forgotten the whole last couple of months since Tem came back to Lockgrove Bay.

Newsflash. I haven't stopped thinking about Tem from the moment I saw her again. But I'm not about to admit that to Zeke. The tosser will use that against me.

He's still talking and I tune back into his words, "And now I don't know what you've done with my best mate. One eighty, man. Grow some balls."

He's riling me up. He knows I'll bite back.

"Yeah, well maybe you should not shoot for goal in every willing chick, Ezekiel," I taunt, using his full name because he hates it so much. His anger is starting to boil over. He hates it when I call him out on being a manwhore.

"At least I'm getting pussy. I bet Tem's told her sexy bestie Lorena how much she wants to fuck you," he remarks with a cocky smirk. I want to smack it off his face again. He's a tosser.

And thats confirmed by the next words that spill out of his mouth, "I've been dreaming of a threesome with them actually."

My anger rises, and I clench the skipping rope in my fist, throwing it on the ground, shoving my hands against Zeke's chest, pushing him to the ground.

"You wouldn't fucking dare!" I roar at him, stepping over him.

He's looking up at me, still with the cocky smirk when he speaks, "You sure? I mean if you don't want her."

"Fuck you, Ezekiel!" I bellow, leaning over him and punching him square in the jaw. He lets out a chuckle, taunting me, "Hit me again. I dare you."

I'm seething. My best mate is a fucking arsehole.

"Hit me or admit you've got feelings for Tempany," he jeers at me.

Loathing Temptation

"I don't! I hate her! And you!" I bellow, hitting him again harder. He doesn't even fight back. And I can't stop myself from laying into him. I hate myself. I'm not this guy.

I'm about to punch the cocky bastard in the nose when I feel Miss M step up behind me, grabbing my Guernsey and pulling me away from beating my best mate to a pulp.

"Principals office now, Ashton," Miss Miller screams at me.

I don't dare look back at Zeke as I walk off, even when I hear Miss Miller say, "Lorena can you take Zeke to first aid?"

I've fucked up. I'm turning into him.

Getting to the principals' office I'm shocked by what I find. Shocked about who is walking out of Ms Masters office in the middle of the school day. Well, not completely shocked, but still I'm not expecting to see my dad at school; looking dishevelled. The walk of shame look. The I've just fucked someone look.

It makes me want to chunder, projectile style.

He stops just outside the office door, glaring at me.

"What are you doing here Ashton?" he asks with a hint of anger in his voice.

"Showed Zeke that he's a tosser with my fists. What are you doing here daddy?"

"Nothing. Just leaving," he says, guilt lacing his tone. He knows I've caught him out.

"Right," I jeer. "More like coming. Coming inside principal Masters' pussy."

As usual, he can't control his anger, and berates me, "What did you just say, boy?"

Caz May

I hate when he calls me boy. It makes me feel four feet tall. Makes me feel like I'm that eight-year-old getting my first beating. Today though, I puff my chest out, ready to knock him down a peg.

"I know dad. I know your dirty little secret."

He huffs at me, blowing out an exasperated breath. I continue with an accusing tone, "Your fucking principal Masters."

I can see that his blood is boiling. But still, I go on, "I'm sure the school board would love to hear all about it."

And then he shocks me, not by raising his fist but with his calm words, laced with a threat, "Tell them, son. And bye bye all you care about."

He starts to walk away and I reach down to open the office door.

"Sure dad. I'll see you after school."

After dad fucks off down the hallway I open the door fully to go into Ms Masters office. Being in here again makes bile rise in my throat and I'm trying not to think about how she was fucking my dad—probably over her desk—mere minutes ago.

I sit in the tub chair, not looking up at her. I can tell she's shaking her head in disappointment. I couldn't give a rats arse though, even when she speaks my care factor is zero.

"Ashton, I'm disappointed in you. I can't write you the recommendation letter for RMIT if you continue with this destructive behaviour."

This time I do look up at her, giving her dagger eyes.

"Well, I don't really care Miss Masters," I start, glaring at her to rile her up. I know I get to her, just as much as my dad does.

Loathing Temptation

"And if you don't write the letter, I'll tell the school board you're fucking my dad to get his money."

Shock paints her face. Her mouth falls open, a worried whimper escaping.

"Thought that might be the ticket," I jeer, standing up, out of the chair, and slapping my arse cheekily before walking out.

Thirty-Six
Tempany

*A*fter a horrible day at school, I let myself into the house, dumping my bag by the door. Ashton's backpack is already there which means he's home already from basketball training.

For the past couple of weeks other than having to see him at school, I've been avoiding him, and I really don't want to see him because he's been a suggestive dickhead taunting me and making me feel things for him I shouldn't.

I hate that his teasing—his clear hatred—towards me makes butterflies dance in my stomach and my knickers feel damp with my desire for him.

Loathing Temptation

I'm about to head up to my room, but my stomach is rumbling a protest because I haven't eaten since recess. I'd had to get in some extra practice of the song for the eisteddfod, as I'm still not hitting the high notes.

I can hear Ashton's voice as I head into the kitchen. And walking into the open plan kitchen I find him sitting on the counter in only his basketball Guernsey with his phone to his ear.

I reach out to grab an apple from the bowl on the island bench and he sticks his tongue out at me, winking suggestively when he puts his phone down beside him on the bench.

He looks absolutely gorgeous, and I can't help licking my lips wondering if he's wearing anything under the Guernsey. It's halfway up his thighs, and his legs are open slightly.

I'm practically drooling, so take a bite of my apple, not able to stop staring at him or move out of the kitchen.

He winks at me again.

"You got a problem, temptress? Or you just like staring at me?"

Of course, I like—love—staring at him. But I hate his taunts and his cocky attitude. My heart is hammering in my chest, just from being in the same room as him, but I cannot deal with the tension for a moment longer.

I need to confront him and find out why he's still being such a dick to me. Taking another bite of my apple, I step into the kitchen more, stopping in front of his legs, but far enough away that he can't quite reach me.

Taking a deep breath, I exhale and ask, "Why Ashton?"

It's a simple question, and I'm worried it doesn't ask what I need to know. But I don't know what else to ask.

He lets out a chuckle, shifting on the bench a little.

"You're my stepsister Tempany," he reminds me, matter of factly, before leaning forward and whispering close to my lips, "And you forget that I loathe you."

He shifts back, and I take a step forward, now practically standing in between his open legs.

"But why?" I ask, gulping and telling myself to find more words. "I haven't done anything wrong."

He chuckles again, and my eyes are drawn to his Adam's apple, making the tingles rush through my body. I need to find more words. To get him to see how angry he makes me.

"And you didn't think about me being your stepsister when you kissed me and touched me."

His hands press against the bench like he doesn't know where to put them and he takes a deep breath in.

"I hate you because you ruined my life Tempany. You made my dad ruin my life."

His words and the anger in his tone hurt. Really hurt and my anger flares, giving me a feeling of brazenness.

"Fuck you, Ashton," I yell at him, locking my eyes on his.

His stormy eyes light up with a flash of desire, and he bites back, "You want me to fuck you temptress?"

My whole body tingles with his question. And he squeezes his thighs to cage me in. I'm salivating and my breathing has quickened contemplating my answer for a moment.

"Yes," I mutter softly, leaning into him so my answer lands on his lips.

Loathing Temptation

"Mmm, temptress," he purrs, a little breathless which I'm sure means he's turned on. I don't get to think about that anymore or say anything before his hand is in my hair, yanking me closer.

He kisses me again, devouring my mouth and letting out moans that send a shockwave of pleasure through me.

Kissing Ashton is a rush, an outta body euphoric feeling that I want to feel over and over. His lips on mine feel electric, and he bites down on my lip, pulling it back between his teeth, before soothing the sting with his tongue. I could get so used to kissing him because when he's kissing me it feels like he doesn't hate me.

But right when I think that maybe he doesn't hate me like he keeps telling me, he pulls away from the kiss, pushing a hand against my chest and shoving me away.

"Fuck off Tempany! Ava's home."

Tears sting my eyes, and without even looking at him, I rush out to my room, bumping into Ava just outside the archway to the kitchen. She looks at me with concern, but I don't say anything.

The tears are pouring down my cheeks now, and I just want to run up the stairs to my room, and let them out onto my pillow.

I want to hate Ashton. But I don't.

I'm falling for my stepbrother, and he hates me.

Thirty-Seven

Ashton

Since kissing Tem in the kitchen, and shoving her away because my dick was so fucking hard—and I was commando—under my Guernsey I've barely seen her. She's been practising her eisteddfod piece after school with Zeke, so our usual arvo call of duty sessions haven't been happening.

And what sucks is that I'm missing my best mate, but also that I'm jealous he's getting to spend time with Tempany. He's probably putting moves on her, and I'm not there to stop him.

But he could actually be with her, not like me. She's my stepsister. And that means I can't want her, even if Ash Jnr is a traitorous bastard and isn't getting the message that Tempany is forbidden.

Loathing Temptation

Sitting on the couch, I'm trying to concentrate on a game of COD, but Ava is sitting next to me with a book and won't stop looking up at me. I can see her staring out of the corner of my eye.

"You ok Av's?" I ask, turning slightly to meet her eyes that look up at me from her book.

She smiles at me, cheekily and blurts out a question, "Have you got feelings for her?"

I don't respond for a moment, gulping.

"Ashy, do you have feelings for Te?" she asks again.

I pause the game, clutching the controller in my grip, so hard my knuckles go white.

I shake my head.

"No," I mutter, biting down on my lip.

Ava can usually see right through me, and right now is no exception. She lets out a giggle.

"Could've fooled me brother. I've seen how you look at her," my sister tells me, making images of Tem sitting across from me at the dinner table flash in my mind.

I don't reply, and Ava continues, "And I know you were kissing her in the kitchen the other day."

My breath catches in my chest. I knew Ava had come home, but I didn't know she was so close that she could have seen the hot kiss Tem and I shared. I'd not been able to get that kiss to leave my mind.

Tem kissing me, fuck it gets to me.

"You saw nothing, Ava," I snap.

Ava giggles, poking me in the arm.

"I saw you kissing Te, Ashy. Admit it and I won't tell mum."

Damn my cheeky little sister.

"Fine, I've kissed her. You happy?"

"Nope." Ava laughs, clearly teasing me.

"You're a devil, Ava Darby," I jeer at her, poking her playfully.

"You love me and you love Tempany," she jeers at me, giggling.

I go back to playing my game, thinking about my little sisters' words. I can't love Tem. She gets to me and is definitely under my skin, but love, fuck nah.

I shake the thoughts away, telling myself that *'I hate her, I hate Tempany.'*

Ava's teasing about my feelings had really gotten to me. Thoughts of Tem are never far from my mind as it is and my little sister calling me out on my feelings is stirring up an odd feeling in my guts. It's hard to admit to myself, but I've been a prick. All I want though is to taunt Tem more and be with her more, even though it's wrong. Forbidden has never felt so good.

Walking into school early, I make sure no one is around before sneaking into principal Masters' office. I can't believe her door has no lock on it, especially when she likes to fuck people she shouldn't on her desk.

Spotting the filing cabinet in the corner, I open it, flipping through the student files until I find Tempany's. Grabbing it out I flick through the files for the details of her locker.

2142. Yeah, I'm not going to fucking remember that.

Loathing Temptation

I glance to Ms Masters desk, laughing when I see the heart-shaped popup post-it note dispenser. She's certainly a weird one. Pulling out a note, I also grab a pencil and write the combination down before shoving the note in my pocket and putting the file back in the filing cabinet.

Leaving the office, I'm feeling kinda nervous about what I'm about to do. Tem probably hates me for being an arsehole, and kissing her and then ignoring her. And getting to her locker after a quick trip to mine to grab the flowers I fumble with the lock, having to do the combination three times before the lock clicks to open.

I put the small bunch of unfortunately slightly now wilted peach, orange and white roses in her locker, resting them on top of a pile of books with a note attached to the stems.

It certainly doesn't look pretty. I used so much sticky tape around the stems to keep them together, and the damn thorns had to fight me, so the white paper for the note has a couple of drops of my blood on it. I should have re-written the note, but that would've been too much effort.

I close her locker, scooting back down the hallway to mine when the bell goes.

Students start filing in, and I stand at the end of the locker bay waiting for Tempany to walk in. I want to watch her when she opens her locker. Weird I know, but I'm kinda getting excited just thinking about her reading my note.

Thankfully I don't have to wait long before she's at her locker. Her outfit is fucking sexy; black leggings and an oversized jumper that just covers her arse.

I literally can't tear my eyes away, watching her opening her locker. She grabs the roses out, glancing around for a moment. She looks horrified when her eyes scan the note but then she smiles, clutching the roses to her chest and sniffing them.

Carefully she puts them back inside her locker, grabbing out a book before she walks away, her eyes scanning the hallway as though she's looking for me.

I don't know how to feel about her reaction and have no idea whether she'll let me fuck her, but god do I want to.

I need to fuck her to fuck away any thought of feelings I might have for her.

Loathing Temptation

Thirty-Eight
Tempany

O pening my locker my eyes instantly drop to the bunch of roses with a note wrapped around the stem.

Grabbing them I unwrap the note, gulping back the bile that threatens to rise in my throat when I stare at it. There's a couple of droplets of blood on the white paper, and I'm a little disgusted by that, more so when I read the words my stepbrother has written in his scrawly handwriting.

I loathe you Tempany.
But I want to fuck you hard until you scream my name.
Ashton

I'm disgusted, but the tingly feeling is also rushing through me. I've thought about *'fucking'* Ashton way too much. But even though we've kissed and fooled around, I honestly didn't even want to entertain the thought that Ashton would want anything more from me.

Clutching the roses to my chest for a moment I sniff them, inhaling the sweet fragrance whilst looking around for Ashton, but I can't see him nearby.

Shrugging I put the roses back inside my locker and grab out my books for class. The first bell sounds and I head down the hallway to music class.

Walking in before the second bell I'm surprised to find Zeke is already in class, sitting back on a chair with his hands behind his head, and his legs crossed at the ankles. His presence commands the whole room and when his eyes graze over my outfit he gives me a wink.

He drops his hands to his lap, watching me walk in. I know I'm smiling like an idiot from Ashton leaving me flowers in my locker.

Zeke laughs when I get closer.

Loathing Temptation

"Tem, baby. You look happy," he remarks, giving me another wink that is very suggestive. "Did you get some dick?" he asks

"No," I mutter sitting down next to him and slapping a hand across his cheek for being a dickhead. Him calling me *baby* is odd, and I wonder for a moment what in the world has gotten into him.

Plus I'm also wondering about things with him and Lorena. She hasn't mentioned anything else about him lately, and I make a mental note to ask what's going on with them.

Zeke lets out a muffled screech of pain, then chuckles with a cocky grin on his face.

"Tem...burn baby," he taunts, nodding towards his crotch. "You can have my dick if you want it. No need to fight me."

I huff, scooting my chair away when a substitute teacher walks into the room and glances around like he's lost.

I turn my chair around so I'm not facing Zeke anymore. Him being sexually suggestive is really confusing and really odd.

He kicks my chair, his foot shoving into the plastic with a thump. I turn around to give him dagger eyes.

"Fuck you, Ezekiel," I spit at him, shocked that I let *fuck* spill out of my mouth so angrily.

His eyes light up and he winks at me, again with his stupid suggestive cocky smirk.

"Anytime baby. But I know you really want Ashton's dick."

Just the thought of Ashton's dick makes me gulp and a blush rises up my cheeks, rendering me tongue-tied.

Zeke decides my lack of words means he can tease me more. "I know you've sucked him, Tem. So jelly baby."

I glare at him, completely shocked.

"Stop, Zeke!" I seethe, getting up and raising my hand to slap him again. The substitute teacher is standing behind the desk, glaring at us. We're most definitely in trouble. And it makes my stomach turn.

"Excuse me, what is going on?" the teacher questions loudly, making his presence in the room known.

"Oh, nothing sir," Zeke says, too polite for him. "Except for my girl here about to give my dick some attention under the table."

I'm absolutely outraged by his suggestion, and without thinking I raise my leg, kneeing him in the crotch. And he bellows out an extremely loud, "Fuck, Tem!"

"I'm not your girl Ezekiel!" I scream at him, hearing our classmates gasping around us, and laughing as well.

Zeke stands up clutching his balls.

"Yeah, thank fuck," he says with a moan, before yelling right in my face, "Go fuck Ashton!"

The teacher is seething. "Both of you," he bellows, pointing at us in turn. "Out now! Detention now!"

I grab my books and trudge towards the door, looking back to give Zeke an up yours. I rush out of the classroom then with him hobbling behind me.

"Tem, wait, please. I'm sorry," he calls out after me, trying to catch up whilst still clutching his crotch.

I stop at the door to detention, standing with my back against it when he steps up to me; a little to close.

"Why Zeke?" I ask softly.

"Because I'm a dick," he tells me, lacing his tone with sincerity that I'm not sure is genuine. "And I'm sorry, but music class with a sub is like an hour of hell."

Loathing Temptation

"So is detention. I've never had detention."

He steps closer to me, into my personal space, placing one hand above my head with his long legs outstretched behind him so the door is taking his weight. He leans in towards me a little more, and panic rises in my chest. *Is he going to kiss me?*

My chest rises with a sharp breath. Having Zeke this close is weird. He's hot yes, but he's not my stepbrother.

"First time for everything, baby, " he says with his cocky suggestive tone. "And don't worry I won't tell Ash you're into me."

"Am not. I...I..." I stutter out my words. I'm such an idiot.

He laughs and the door opens behind me, making me stumble back into the detention room.

Zeke follows me in and says teasingly, "I know, Tem. You dig Ashton. I'm just teasing you."

I huff, annoyed when I head into the room and sit down. Zeke steps up to Miss Miller sitting behind the desk at the front of the room.

I hear Miss Miller ask, "What are you both in for?"

Zeke chuckles, looking at me for a moment, his cocky smirk on his face again when he replies to Miss Miller, "I tried to get Tempany to suck my dick."

Miss Miller stifles a laugh.

"I'm sure that's not all Ezekiel," Miss Miller enquires, which makes Zeke seem a little shy for a moment.

"Wasn't Miss M. She gave me a knee to the balls instead and the sub didn't like our little lovers spat when I cursed out."

Miss Miller sniggers. "Right, well I don't blame him, Ezekiel. But Tempany shouldn't be here because of your crass attitude."

He winks at me, before looking back to Miss Miller, and pushing me under the bus.

"She swore though Miss M. She literally said fuck you, Ezekiel."

Miss M stands up, her anger flaring and she raises her voice at Zeke, "Sit down Ezekiel! And shut the hell up for the next hour. You've just landed yourself three after school detentions."

"Oh come on Miss M. I only said fuck." He winks at her.

I can't believe what I'm witnessing. Zeke is pushing Miss Miller to her limits. She looks like she actually wants to hit him.

"Four Ezekiel!" she roars, pointing towards an empty chair.

He shies away, about to sit down next to me when Miss Miller points to the other side of the room. She gives me an apologetic smile when Zeke sits down, slumping in the chair and not looking across at me.

He's a dickhead, and for the next half an hour I sit there thinking of all the things I want to do to Zeke, like throwing my unicorn pencil case at his head. And also hoping that I'm not going to be in mega trouble when I get home and dad finds out I had my first ever detention, all because of my stepbrother's crass, annoying best friend being an idiot.

Loathing Temptation

Thirty-Nine

Ashton

Driving home from dad's my eye and my jaw are smarting so bad I can barely see straight. After failing the most recent maths test, I should've just avoided my check in with him. But now he's fucking my principal like a fucking bunny on a damn mission, I was bound to run into him again at school so getting the beating away from prying eyes was inevitable.

I want to kill the motherfucker so fucking much. The world wouldn't miss Fidel Castello. But my little sister and mum would probably miss me if I went to jail. And who knows maybe even Tempany would miss me, but I doubt that.

She's so damn hot and cold with me. Wants me—tempts me—one day and then ignores me the next.

She's definitely pure, because she acts like a frigid bitch most of the time. And I hate that because of that not wanting me attitude—and her sexy outfits—that I want her, all of her like my next damn breath.

I don't like this feeling. It makes my dick ache for her, and also makes my heart hammer in my chest.

Pulling into the driveway, I cut the engine of the Camaro, pocketing my keys and heading straight inside to the bathroom.

I take in my appearance in the mirror, nearly chundering from the sight of my messed up face. The black eye is already clearly visible, and my eyes are bloodshot.

There's a gash on my cheek that looks nasty, blood dried at the edges. Touching it, the pain rips through me again, the image of his fist with the hideous sharp knuckle dusters on his fingers hitting my face.

Grabbing a face washer I wet it under a stream of warm water, when I hear footsteps that stop at the bathroom door. I should have fucking shut it.

Looking towards the door, I find my temptress standing in the doorjamb, her face aghast.

She steps into the bathroom, and I want to push her away, but I don't have the strength right now.

"What happened?" she asks, softly, staring at me like she actually cares. I shouldn't tell her. But the way she's looking at me, it's hitting me right in the damn feels.

"My prick of father, Tempany," I shout at her, and her face falls. She's about to cry, and about to reach out and touch me.

Loathing Temptation

I can't let her. If she touches me now, I'll fucking shatter.

"Fuck off and leave me alone!" I roar, my eyes boring into hers, pleading her to listen.

"Your dad did this to you?" she asks, again in the same soft meek voice.

I clench my fists, squeezing the wet face washer so much it's practically dry.

"Yes," I tell her, barely a whisper before I raise my voice, "Now fuck off!"

She doesn't leave. But steps a little closer to me.

"Why Ashton?"

Seriously, can she just fuck off.

"Because..." I start looking back at the mirror. Her eyes meet mine in the reflection of us in the glass, and I can see the tears trying to break free. She's crying now. But she'd probably not give a flying fuck if I told her the truth.

She acts like she's forgotten about what happened ten years ago. But she remembered me. It doesn't make any fucking sense.

"Forget it," I snap loudly. "I'm not going to share my fucked up life with you."

Her hand reaches down to grab mine, our fingers brushing lightly against each other. And it sends that rush through me.

No, and no. I can't let her in now.

"I can help," she suggests with a smile trying to curve her lips.

I snatch my hand away, seething.

"No you can't!" I bellow, throwing the face washer at her. "You're the reason he does this to me!"

She takes a step back, biting down on her lip and sobbing, "What? What do you mean? How?"

She's looking at me worriedly, and confused, like she's trying to remember. And like her heart is breaking along with mine.

I want to tell her, and I'm about to open my mouth to tell her but she rushes out of the bathroom in tears.

Fuck, I'm an arsehole.

After cleaning up the gash on my face I head out of the bathroom, and instead of heading into my own room I go into Tem's. She's lying on her bed, clutching her pillow and sobbing into it. I hate that I've made her cry. And thats a first for me.

I sit on the bed, and she looks up at me when I speak, "Temptress, I'm sorry," I tell her, rubbing my fingers up and down her bare arm. She murmurs softly, but doesn't say anything.

My heart is hammering in my chest when I continue, "I...um...my dad beats me. I can't do anything right. And it's been happening since I was a kid." The words all come out so fast I'm out of breath, gulping in air to calm myself.

Tem moves to sit up against the headboard, her glassy eyes looking straight through me.

"But what do I have to do with it?"she asks, grabbing my hand. Her touch feels amazing. My breath hitches, and I ask her worriedly, "You don't remember much from before you left?"

She shakes her head, biting down on her lip nervously, before she wipes a tear away from her cheek with the hand that isn't gripping mine tightly.

"No, I...I blocked it all out. What happened to me before we left. Why dad left mum. Everything but you," she confesses, a blush colouring her cheeks.

"Me? You telling me you thought about me?" I ask, with a hint of teasing in my tone.

"Everyday, Simba."

I laugh, feeling a pang of desire hitting me.

"Simba?" I ask with a wink.

She smiles at me.

"Yeah, you're my lion, Ashton. My protector. Thinking of you got me through."

I can't believe her words. She'd thought about me these past ten years, for completely different reasons than I've thought about her. And I feel like the biggest arsehole of the century.

"Shit Tempany. I...fuck...I..."

There isn't anything else to say, so instead I lean in closer to her, kissing her, and letting the desire for her take over. She murmurs against my lips, asking for more. Her hand still clutching mine yanks me down and I fall on top of her, still kissing her like I need her to survive.

I deepen the kiss, my tongue licking her lips. I can feel her heart beating rapidly against my own crazy heartbeat. And I can't...

Breaking the kiss, I pull back, glaring at her for a moment before I stand up from her bed and walk out of her bedroom angry with myself.

I'd thought the first time I'd kissed her was the most epic kiss of my life, but that was so much more. That kiss was laced with feelings I'm not sure I'm ready to feel.

Feelings I shouldn't feel for my temptress of a stepsister.

Forty

Tempany

T ears break through, cascading down my cheeks the moment Ashton walks out my bedroom door.

A million and one thoughts are crashing into my mind, thinking back to before I left Lockgrove Bay ten years ago. The memories are painful, him—that horrible man with the dark eyes—touching me, his words telling me to be a 'good girl' and he'll reward me. And then the memories of playing basketball with Ashton. Being with him was the only time I could block out the horror of being at home, around my mum and him. Dad had left because mum was drinking herself into oblivion, and when she drank she didn't know who he was. That was when he—the dark eyed man—came over and said those words to me, always after he'd been loudly having sex with mum in her bedroom with the door open. The memories are hitting me hard.

I pull my covers back, crawling underneath and letting the tears fall, trying to think of the good memories. The ones with Ashton. With the boy who made the butterflies flit in my stomach. The only memories that come to me though make my heart shatter.

I can see that day in my mind, taking his basketball before Mum called out my name from across the park. I didn't really mean to take it, but I knew we were leaving this time, for good. And my heart was hurting. I just wanted something to remember him by. And I'd wanted to give him a kiss goodbye. He made me giddy when I was seven, and now he owns my heart, even though he doesn't deserve it.

Without a doubt, I'm in love with Ashton. And I have been since the day I first laid eyes on him, playing basketball when I was six.

I close my eyes then, wondering for a moment if I should go in and tell him that I remember taking his basketball. I wonder if I should ask him more about his dad beating him, but it's clear he's not ready to share, so I'm not going to pry.

Closing my eyes, I let the tears fall down my cheeks, crying myself to sleep from the painful memories of the past and the longing for a future I can't have.

After waking up from a horrible sleep, barely getting in a few hours where the memories didn't haunt me I'm wandering around school like a zombie. I'm avoiding Ashton, but he's always there glaring at me, being suggestive with his winks and sticking his tongue out at me. He looks wickedly gorgeous when he does that, and it makes me think of kissing him, his tongue lacing with mine.

But thinking of kissing him—and wanting more with him— makes my heart hurt. I want more from him, but I know I can't have that.

Thankfully I only have one class with him, and for the rest of the day I hide out in the library, reading. Lorena isn't at school again, but when I'd spoken to her last she was as sick as a dog with the flu. I sent flowers and her fave choccies over and she sent me back a selfie of her practically inhaling the chocolates.

Rubbing my eyes I amble into the house after school. Ashton and Zeke are on the couch playing video games. Hearing me come inside, Zeke's head turns to me and they both eye me. My eyes are stinging and I'm about to burst into tears.

My feet feel glued to the floor. I hate this feeling. But I can't move.

"Oh, Tem, why you crying baby?" Zeke jeers at me giving me his signature wink and cocky smirk. The tears have streaked my cheeks now, and if I felt better I'd be slapping him again.

But I don't have the energy to do that or even care about what he's saying.

Ashton glares at him like he's giving his best friend *'A how you dare call her that look.'* That makes my heart skip a beat.

"Shit day," I mutter as I head closer to the staircase.

Zeke nods suggestively at Ashton.

"We can make it better, hey Ash?" he jeers again.

Loathing Temptation

Ashton's eyes dart between his best friend and me, but he doesn't respond to Zeke's taunt.

He turns away, going back to playing his video game.

Zeke gives me a slight smile before doing the same as his best mate. I rush upstairs to my room, throwing my backpack on the bed and sitting down with it at my feet.

I'm upset with myself for being in love with Ashton when he doesn't give a shit about me, even after everything we've been through, in the past before I left and in these past couple of months since I've been back.

It annoys me that he's a completely different person around his best mate. He's not the same guy who gives me sweet kisses that make me want to melt. But then again, he's not the same sweet boy I left behind on the basketball court ten years ago either.

He grew up to be an arsehole. And I hate that I want him so much. That I love him so much.

Wiping my arm across my face, I tell myself to get it together. I need to stop crying over Ashton Castello.

Getting out my homework from my bag—my English workbook—a tear drops onto the page, right where I've written I♡ Ashton. Why do I have to be so desperately in love with him?

I'm writing it on my books like a lovesick fool. I'm such an idiot.

Picking it up, I let out a scream and throw the book across the room.

Fuck him!

My stepbrother can go to hell.

Forty-One

Ashton

Zeke is giving me side eye. He clearly wants to say something, and deliberately makes his character die, before he questions me suddenly, "You right mate?"

"No, you fucking douche," I tell him, looking at him out of the corner of my eye. "I hate you talking about Tem that way."

The fucker has the gall to laugh, before replying cockily, "Like what? Teasing her? Or calling her baby?"

"Calling her baby," I tell him, anger in my tone. "She's not your girl."

Again he laughs, like a cocky arsehole. I want to fucking slap him.

Loathing Temptation

"And what? She's yours? You actually told her how you feel?" he taunts me.

"No," I snap, shaking my head. "Well, if you mean that I've told her I hate her, then yes."

He pauses the game, shifting closer to me on the couch and slaps me around the ears, his open palm slapping against my head.

"You're a fucking idiot Ash," he booms out. "If you hate her then why are you acting like a pussy whipped wanker?"

I shift back, leaning my back against the armrest.

God, I want to slap him back so fucking hard.

"I'm not acting like anything," I protest. "You're the only wanker here. You need to grow the fuck up and stop with the sexual shit every damn second."

His eyes boggle at me, his face aghast with shock that I'm calling him out on his bullshit for once.

"I've had enough of your shit, especially about Tem," I bellow at him.

He lets out his annoying as shit chuckle again, and god I wanna shut him up with a fist to the fucking face.

"Damn man. You've got it so bad. Seriously get up to her damn room, and fuck her brains out."

That's it! I'm fucking livid!

Standing up, I throw my controller on the floor, grabbing Zeke by the shirt and pulling him up to his feet. He's shitting himself, and if I wasn't so fucking angry I'd be cacking myself laughing.

With my teeth clenched I seethe in his face, "Doing that would make me an arsehole. And I won't be one to her anymore."

Zeke lets out a grunt and I let go of his shirt shoving him back towards the couch. Again he laughs, berating me with his cocky grin, even though seconds ago he was about to shit his daks.

"You are an arsehole, Ashton," he informs me like it's news to me. "Don't hide from it," he taunts, stepping around the coffee table like a scared little mouse.

I shake my head.

"Yeah, Nah, her dad is an arsehole for what he did. Leaving her. And I'm not going to be with her when I'll turn out to be an arsehole too," I tell him, suddenly feeling guilty for how much of an arsehole I've been towards Tem since she came home.

"Whatever, dickwad...I'm out. Man up."

He strolls out then, leaving me to think about his words.

Stepping into the kitchen after an early run, I'm surprised to find Tempany sitting at the breakfast bar eating fruit loops.

"Hey," I greet her.

She grunts at me, spooning more of the fruit loops into her mouth.

"Oh, it's like that is it temptress?" I jeer, leaning on the bench and dipping my finger into the bowl.

I put the milk covered finger in my mouth, moaning. "Mmm, tastes good, but you know what tastes better, temptress?"

Again she grunts, her mouth falling open watching me sucking my finger. "Yeah, your pussy, temptress," I tell her with a laugh and a smirk.

Loathing Temptation

"Eww, Ashton! Seriously, stop!" she yells at me before scooting the bar stool back, and grabbing her bowl with two hands.

She turns her back on me for a moment, and I step closer to the fridge to get out some orange juice. With my back turned, I feel her step up behind me, but I don't move, until I feel the cold milk and the sticky fruit loops dripping down my back.

"Whoops," Tem says, laughing.

Oh no she fucking didn't!

"What the fuck temptress!"

She laughs again, and even though I'm pissed with her it makes my stomach flip flop with desire for her. *Fuck me dead.*

"It seemed like you wanted some of my breakfast. And I slipped."

"Oh right, well don't let it happen again."

"Oh, I wouldn't dare. But sorry if you did want some fruit loops."

"Huh?"

"You'll have to eat them off the floor. I ate them all," she tells me with a sweet smile, laughing when she puts her bowl in the sink and saunters off to get dressed. It's then I realise that she's wearing some sexy nightie and has nothing on underneath.

Ash Jnr jolts in my daks, and I curse myself for being such a dick again. I could have pushed her up against the counter and tasted her for breakfast.

What a damn waste, but I have to admit she got me back. And it turns me on so bad that my temptress is giving me sass back.

Forty-Two

Ashton

For the past few weeks, I've barely seen Tem, and she's been constantly on my mind. I know I've been an arsehole to her, especially when I cursed out at her about her dad being an arsehole because he left her with her mum.

The look on her face broke me, fucking shattered me. It was like I literally tore her heart out of her chest and was holding it bleeding in my hand. I'd wanted to kiss her, tell I'm sorry and I wanted to tell her about my own arsehole of a father, but she screamed at me, running out of the house with tears streaming down her cheeks.

Yeah, I could've gone after her, because I knew exactly where she went. The basketball court. But I didn't go after her because

I'm an arsehole. Dickhead of the century. And a downright fool of epic proportions when it comes to her.

I need to make it up to her. I need to apologise, even if she doesn't accept it. I—Ashton Castello—need to fall to my knees for her.

When I get home from school, she's not in her room, which is perfect as it gives me time to put my plan into action.

From the kitchen, I grab the chicken shears—hoping they'll be sharp enough—and I head out the back door to the rose garden.

Taking a few moments I bend down and smell the roses. So cliched I know, but I kinda like—ok I love the smell—of roses. They remind me of her, of Tempany.

And inhaling the deep red ones my mind fills with thinking about our kisses, and I know that this time I need to leave her a red rose.

I don't want the rose to bite me this time, so using the shears I snip off the big thorns before cutting the rose. It's a large open blossom, and it smells so damn good. I could get high off it, dreaming of going all the way with Tem. I'm kinda secretly hoping this little gesture will get me at least a kiss, but all the way I'd be in rose-orgasmic heaven. I want to fuck my temptresses brains out, whilst inhaling her tempting smell.

With the rose in hand, I go inside, creeping into her bedroom.

I can hear the shower, which possibly means she's home and I don't have much time. Her English workbook is open on her bed and I rip a page out. There are other pages ripped out already, so she won't miss the one I'm holding in my hand, but I do wonder for a moment why she would have ripped out pages of her workbook when it seems like she keeps all of her things like that perfect.

I sneak a pen from the ugly as shit unicorn pencil case that's fallen out of her open backpack and I scrawl out a note to her.

Tem, my temptress.
I'm sorry you had to see my thorns.
Ashton xxx

Quickly I put everything back in place, as though I haven't touched it, leaving the red rose and the note on her pillow.

Stepping out of her room, I see her coming from the bathroom in her oversized jumper again, rubbing her hair with a towel.

She doesn't look at me, and my heart falls. I head into my room, and try to occupy myself with doing homework.

I'm hoping she comes in to tell me that she's accepted my apology, but when fifteen minutes pass I go out to get a drink and find her door is closed.

Message received, temptress. I'm an arsehole. And my apology has not been accepted.

Loathing Temptation

Forty-Three

Tempany

I'd been moping around the house for a week, giving Ashton the silent treatment since he left the rose and note on my pillow.

He hadn't made much of an effort after that to talk to me or anything. We just lived in the same house, walking around on eggshells and not saying one word to each other. He wasn't doing his suggestive gestures, instead, he just smiled at me every time we were in the same room. And it makes my heart beat so hard as well as the butterflies flit in my stomach.

But I hate being the lovesick fool, pining after him when he clearly doesn't love me back.

Caz May

We also need to talk about the past, about the day I left because the fact I took his ball, for something to remember him by obviously bothers him for some stupid reason. It's just a basketball.

Even so, I got him a new one, a truce, peace offering. I'd been nervous about giving it to him all week, more so now I'm clutching it to my chest and about to give it to him. Thankfully Zeke isn't over for their usual Saturday afternoon video games and Ashton is sitting alone on the couch, playing a basketball game; of all things

Stepping up behind the couch, I take in a deep breath and softly say, "Hey Ashton."

He turns to look at me, pausing his game. There's a massive lump in my throat. And I'm about to bolt from the room and throw the ball at him in a crazed panic.

Why did I think this was a good idea?

He smiles at me. And I'm practically a puddle on the floor.

"Hi Temptress," he purrs at me, making my heart pound even harder.

He eyes the ball, looking at it and then up at me. Swallowing the lump in my throat I blurt out, "I got you a new basketball."

I go to hand it to him, but he laughs. And then stands up from the couch. He's angry for some crazy reason and leaning against the back of the couch he's in my face and seethes at me, "Who fucking cares, Tem. Giving me this now doesn't make up for taking my ball ten years ago."

I feel the tears sting my eyes. And when he glares at me, cutting into me with his intense gaze I'm crying. And I'm angry now too. I was only trying to be nice. To apologise, make amends for something that's obviously caused him pain, but he's too much

Loathing Temptation

of an arse to care. I'm regretting the words I wrote on it with black sharpie now.

"Fuck you, Ashton!" I scream at him, throwing the ball at him and running up to my room without giving him a moment to respond.

Ashton Castello just stomped on my heart.

Why do I love him so much?

Forty-Four

Ashton

The basketball is at my feet, and I picking it up I notice the words she wrote on it in black sharpie. A pang of annoyance hits me that she wrote on a brand new basketball, but actually reading the words is a kick in the guts and the damn feels.

I'm sorry Ashton. Forgive me.
Because...I remember why I took your ball
that day. And I love you. Tempany xxx

Loathing Temptation

In between my palms, I squeeze the ball hard, emotions rushing through me that I'm to scared to feel. It's anger, frustration, lust and fuck, *'love'* maybe.

Holding the ball under my arm I charge up the stairs, barging into her room without knocking on the door.

She's lying down on her bed, sobbing. Heading towards the bed, I ask, "Tem do you mean it?" The words come out much calmer than I thought they would, considering my heart is about to burst out of my chest. *Why does she have me in fucking knots?*

"Of course I mean it, Ashton," she says softly, sitting up on the bed and locking her teary eyes on mine.

God, I actually hate seeing her like this, broken because of my selfish words. And I'm tongue-tied...she's in love with me.

Fuck.

I have nothing to say. What is there to say?

I love you too. No, I can't say that.

Tem breaks my silence, still glaring at me, but this time her eyes are darker, as though anger is flaring up inside her.

"But what does it matter? You don't love me."

Dropping the ball, throwing my hands up in the air in frustration I stalk closer to bed, screaming out, "How the fuck do you know that Tem? You in my damn head?"

She bites down on her lip, in nervous panic and mutters through her teeth, "I...um...no...but...you..."

"I what, temptress? Spit it out!"

She doesn't say anything and my anger flares. I need to calm down. I'm going to say something I regret. I'm about to walk out the door, when she stands up, grabbing the hem of my t-shirt, and pulling me against her body.

Against my lips, she whispers, "It's ok. I know you don't love me. But please, kiss me, Simba."

Fuck, fuck and oh fuck.

When she calls me that I want to combust. It gets to me so bad. I'm her motherfucking lion, and fuck, I...I might be in love. *Nah, but who am I to deny her a kiss?*

Brushing her hair back, and tucking a stray strand behind her ear I softly say against her lips, "I'm sorry Tem. Thank you, for the ball and..." I cut my words off, pressing my lips to hers. And just the soft touch of her lips against mine is enough to send my whole world into a tailspin. Electricity, longing, lust, every emotion known to man is coursing through my veins. And Tem moans against my lips, deepening the kiss.

Oh god help me, I'm falling.

She pulls back, yanking at the hem of my T-shirt to pull it over my head. Helping her I discard it, throwing it on the floor by the basketball. She sits down on the bed, and I lay over her, looking down at her and the emotions reflected in her stormy eyes that are drinking me in.

Her finger brushes over my abs, down to my v-line and she giggles.

"You're sexy, Simba."

"Oh really, temptress?"

"Yeah," she replies with a giggle that sends a jolt to Ash Jnr.

"Well, temptress," I say softly, caressing her cheek. "You're beautiful."

Loathing Temptation

She bites her lip in her sweet nervous way. And I'm worried I put my fucking foot in it. But then she softly mutters, "Really? You think I'm beautiful?"

I lean down, so our lips are a breath apart.

"So fucking beautiful, Tempany."

And I don't let her reply, crashing my lips against hers in a hungry *'you're mine'* kiss. Her legs wrap around my arse, pulling me closer and our hips—and my dick and her pussy—rub against each other.

As we kiss, she moans, pulling me under, and I want to tear her clothes off to touch and kiss her everywhere, to make her mine completely. But before I can even suggest that, she's pulling back, panicking and shoving me away.

"Ashton, we have to stop. We can't."

"Why the hell not, Tem?"

"Because our parents are due to be home any minute."

"Oh shit, fuck," I mutter, glancing towards her open bedroom door. I head towards it, to close it, telling her, "I'll just close the door. No biggie."

But she shakes her head at me.

"No, we can't. Dad told me he had something to show me this arvo."

"Oh right. well, um...I" I stutter walking out, even more confused about my feelings and worried about what her dad needs to show her. I still don't trust the guy. But he's making my mum happier than she's been in years.

And Tempany is making me feel happier than I have in years too, but the fact is we can't be together, because of our parents who speaking of are coming in the door, arms full of groceries the very moment I descend the stairs.

Mum looks at me questioningly, and I realise I forgot my shirt in Tem's room.

Fuck. Might as well go to hell now.

Loathing Temptation

Forty-Five

Tempany

*I*t's well and truly dark, getting close to ten when I sneak into Ashton's room. Heading towards his bed, I hear him groan and ask, "Ashton, are you awake?"

"Yeah, Tem. Can't sleep."

I probably shouldn't but I get into bed with him. And I'm surprised when he murmurs pulling me against his body to cuddle me.

"You ok, Temptress?" he asks softly, kissing my forehead.

"Yeah, but we need to talk."

"I know," he murmurs, shifting so we're facing each other. He props himself up on his elbow, looking at me in the glow of moonlight coming in from his window.

Sighing, I take in a deep breath to calm my nerves, my racing heart. This moment feels more intimate than the kisses we've shared.

"So, before I left there was this man. He was kinda my mum's boyfriend and he...he used to touch me inappropriately after he had sex with my mum. It was horrible, and I..." Ashton brushes a hand across my cheek.

"Tem, that's horrible. Is that why your dad left?"

"No, dad left before that because of mum's drinking. But the day I took your basketball, when we left Lockgrove Bay Mum was running from that man because he hit her, and she was sober for once, so she panicked."

"Oh, fuck, Tem. I'm sorry I had no idea."

I can see the hurt and the sincerity in his eyes. And maybe a hint of something else, but I don't let myself even think that Ashton might feel anything like that for me. The possibility of getting my heart broken, despite his sincerity now is still real.

"And Ash," I say softly, grabbing his hand that's resting on the bed between us. "I only took your basketball because I wanted something to remember you by. I didn't mean for it to hurt you or get you in trouble."

"I know Tem, but it did," he tells me, his eyes locking on mine, tears stinging them. "Dad beat me so hard that day because it was like the fifth basketball I'd 'lost' and I blamed you, hated you for that. And when you came back...I...I wanted to hate you, and hate your dad for leaving you."

"I'm sorry Ashton. I honestly had no idea. I shouldn't have taken it."

"It's the past, Tem. Honestly. If it wasn't that my dad would have beaten me for something else. You know he still does that. And I should be apologising. I didn't want you to be in my life or your dad. Because I didn't want him to be just another arsehole who leaves my mum, and me and Av's."

I'm taken aback for a moment, gulping down the lump caught in my throat from Ashton opening up to me. Everything makes sense now, and I'm heartbroken.

"Yeah, he's not an arsehole. He just made a bad choice to not take me with him," I say, squeezing Ashton's hand I'm still holding.

"Yeah, Tem. I get that. And I'm honestly sorry I thought the worst."

"It's ok," I mutter, "it's the past. Everything, even all the stuff with the horrible man is the past, and it's ok now."

He shakes his head at me, pressing a sweet kiss to my forehead. My insides melt.

"It's not. Nothing that happened to you is ok, Temptress."

He's looking at me with longing, maybe even something else and I'm sure he can hear my heartbeat that's so loud from the galloping of my traitorous organ in my chest. I'm so desperately in love with him, and I might regret the choice I'm about to make in the morning, but right now I want to be as close to Ashton as possible. I want all of him—all of him to be mine.

"Simba?" I ask, my lips a breath away from his.

"Yeah, temptress?" he replies, his breath fanning over my face.

"Can you make me forget the past completely?"

He moves back a little, so he can see my eyes, still staring at him in the low light.

"How so, temptress?"

I bite my lip, nervousness, butterflies and tingles taking over my whole body.

"Fuck me please, Simba."

His eyes light up, lighting in his stormy grey orbs.

"Damn Tempany. That sounds so dirty. But only if you're sure?"

I kiss his lips, softly, sweetly, and reply without hesitation, "I'm sure. I want you to fuck me."

"Mmm, Tem," he murmurs, kissing me and taking my breath away. We kiss for what feels like forever, completely consumed by each other. My heart is hammering in my chest.

Breaking the kiss, I'm panting, and Ashton laughs.

"Damn, temptress. Your kisses are like ecstasy."

"Mmm," I moan. "Stop talking, Simba."

I sit up, pulling my nightie over my head and throwing it on the floor. Ashton stares at me, his gaze wandering my body and he smirks, licking his lips.

"Fuck, temptress. Why you been hiding this perfection from me?"

I slap his abs, feeling his skin heat beneath his white t-shirt. "Stop, Ashton."

"Never, temptress. You. Naked. Fucking glorious."

"Well, you naked, Simba. A fucking sight," I taunt, trying not to laugh.

"Oh it's like that is?" he teases, his fingers brushing over my nipples that are at attention from his simmering gaze.

"Yeah, but maybe if I saw the whole package I might like it."

He chuckles, locking his eyes on mine as he yanks his t-shirt off, throwing it aside and crawling on the bed to pin me down.

He kisses me, and whispers against my lips, "I'm going to fucking worship you temptress."

I can't help but let out a little moan of pleasure, my core aching for him. The tension between us is on fire, and I'm going to burn to ashes, for my lion, my Ashton.

Grabbing his dick through the grey trackies I tease, "If you're going to worship me with your dick, I need to see it."

He chuckles again, his whole chest vibrating and he sits up—staring down at me—and yanks his trackies to his knees. He's commando—again, making me wonder if he ever wears jocks—and he stretches back over me to kiss me again, taking my breath away when his dick which is clearly hard rubs against my clit.

Fuck. Yes, fuck.

He breaks the kiss, kicking the trackies off from his ankles.

"Are you honestly sure about this, Tem?"

"Yes, I'm sure. I'm on the pill. I...I get really bad periods."

He laughs, poking me in the stomach with this finger.

"Eww, Tem, I didn't need to hear that. But damn."

"Sorry," I mutter, biting down on my lip. I can't believe this is really happening. I'm going to officially lose my virginity to the hottest guy I know.

He kisses me again, and whispers against my lips, "Temptress, can I fuck you bare?"

I look at him confused. "Huh?"

He laughs again, and I feel like a naive idiot when he replies, "Can I fuck you without a condom?"

"Oh, um, yeah," I stammer. "And please fuck me now. I can't wait any more."

"Fuck, temptress," he curses, before kissing me again, pouring so much emotion into the kiss I swear I'm going to fall apart just from longing.

Still kissing me, he pushes the tip of his dick against my core.

I whimper from the sudden jolt that rushes through me. Ashton breaks the kiss, speaking softly, "You ok? It might hurt. But I'll go slow."

"I'm fine. Please, more, Simba," I beg, cupping his cheeks to bring his face down to mine for a kiss. He slides his dick in further, biting my lip to stifle his moan as he fills me. I feel a hint of pain, my body adjusting to the feeling of having him inside me.

Again he breaks the kiss, staring down at me, as he starts to rock in and out of my core.

"Oh, shit, Ashton," I curse, biting on my lip to try and not moan like a crazed animal. I've never felt something so amazing in my entire life.

"What temptress?"

"It feels so good. Harder, please."

"Mmm, fuck, Tempany. You're going to kill me, slow."

He thrusts in harder, laying still for a moment and giving me another sweet kiss.

"Temptress, feels so fucking good, but would you ride me?"

I tremble at his words, pleasure pulsing through me.

"Really? I...don't know how."

He laughs, but it's sweet. And he grabs my hips, sitting up and pulling me with him so our chests are against each other. His dick

Loathing Temptation

slips out of me and he leans in to whisper in my ear, "Wrap your legs around my arse, temptress, and sit on my dick."

I follow his direction, and...*Oh my God!*

Pushing my body down over his hard dick, pleasure rushes through me. He moans loudly and I shut him up with a kiss.

"Ride my dick, temptress. Up, down, baby."

Moving my hips up and down I find a rhythm, and it's only a few minutes of the most amazing feeling ever before my body starts trembling, my release building.

"That's it, temptress. Come on my dick, baby."

I ride him harder, biting my lip to stifle my moans of pleasure, and reaching my peak suddenly I come hard, bearing down on him inside me, as he kisses me, his tongue lacing with mine to silence my illicit moan. Breaking the kiss, he pumps his dick inside me hard, calling out, "Fuck Temptress. Fuck, I'm going to come so hard, baby."

He tips his head back then, his whole body vibrating as he pumps inside me one last time, filling me with his hot come, and sending another shiver of pleasure through me.

Wrapping his arms around me, we lay back together on the bed, and he snuggles in close.

"Tem, that was fucking incredible."

I feel a little worried. That it honestly wasn't as good for him— as it was for me—even though he came.

"Really? It was that amazing for you too?"

"Yes, temptress. Absolutely fucking amazing."

I don't reply but snuggle in closer to his chest. He kisses my forehead, and I want to say those three words to him out loud, but I know even though we just shared something so intimate he's not ready to hear them.

Closing my eyes to go to sleep I murmur and say them in my head, *I love you, Ashton Castello.*

Forty-Six

Ashton

My alarm is blaring from my bedside table. Rolling over I slap a hand against it, moaning my annoyance, but then I'm fucking grinning. Tempany is still in my bed—naked—her legs entangled with mine. She murmurs softly, her eyes fluttering open to look at me.

"Morning temptress," I greet her, giving her a soft closed-mouth kiss. She murmurs against my lips.

"Morning, Simba," she purrs at me, making Ash Jnr jolt.

Poking Tem in the belly I laugh, and jeer at her, "Did something happen last night? We appear to both be naked."

Caz May

She smiles, moving to sit in my lap. She leans over me, and I want to fuck her again. Want to slide my aching morning wood right into her wet pussy.

Again she purrs, this time in my ear, "We fucked, Simba."

Hell, her saying fucked sounds so dirty, naughty. I'm about to kiss her again, when she stands up, grabbing her discarded nightie off the floor, pulling it on as she heads towards my bedroom door. She whisper yells, "I'll meet you at your car in twenty minutes."

Groaning I tell Ash Jnr to calm down, sliding out of bed myself, and pulling my trackies on to head for a quick shower before school.

Half an hour later I'm rushing out the door to the Camaro because it took a little longer to calm ash jnr down than I thought it would with thoughts of Tem fucking me last night filling my mind.

"Sorry, sorry," I call out to her and Ava, unlocking the car so they can get in. Tem would normally drive to school herself, but her car had been slipping gears lately and it kinda just made sense to go together. Ava flips the seat back, and I watch Tem slide into the back.

I give her a wink in the rearview mirror, and Ava slides into the passenger seat like a grumpy bear. Turning the ignition over, and reversing out of the driveway I head to school. The tension in the car is thick, and I'm kinda annoyed that I have to take Ava to school as well.

Tem is wearing a short as fuck skirt, with a long button-up jacket over it. And has white knee-high socks on her sexy long

Loathing Temptation

legs. All I can picture is them wrapped around me whilst I fuck her hard. The sex last night was...mind-blowing.

And now I can't stop looking at Tempany. Ava is giving me side eye, and I gulp, knowing she's onto me. Looking at Tem also isn't helping keep Ash Jnr tame. He's threatening to jump out of my daks.

Jolting me out of my Tem focused daze, Ava's voice cuts the tension in the car, "Are you ok, Ashy?"

She's glaring at me now, turning in her seat to look at Tem, when she accusingly asks us both, "Did something happen with you guys?"

"No!" Tem and I both snap at the same time, denying it. I give Tem a sneaky wink in the rearview mirror though and she blushes, smiling at me. And that smile hits me right in the damn feels, and in the damn dick.

Thankfully, we're at school and I pull into my carpark. We're not late, even though I took a little to long to get ready. Ava gets out of the car, and Tem gets in the front seat. She shuts the door and I turn to look at her, giving her a smirk. Ash Jnr is throbbing in my trackies and Tem glances at him, licking her lips.

Leaning over the console, she cups him with her hand, and kisses me, stealing my breath away. It's a sneaky, dirty kiss, her tongue lacing with mine to deepen it, and her hand reaching inside the waistband of my trackies to stroke Ash Jnr.

God her hands feel so fucking good on me. Fuck.

Panting I break the kiss. And she's breathless too but has the same sweet smile on her face that turns me inside out.

Fuck, I think I'm whipped.

"Damn temptress, chill, or I'll be fucking you in the backseat before school starts."

She giggles, gripping Ash Jnr harder. I'm mesmerised by her.

I feel like I honestly can't get enough of her. I'm about to tell her to let Ash Jnr go—stupidly—but only because I'm about to blow my load all over my black trackies and yet again, I'd gone commando, because I had no time to find jocks. But I don't get to say a word when she's leaning further over the console, flipping Ash Jnr out of my trackies, and covering him with her mouth.

Her tongue teases the tip, licking and tasting the pre-cum that's leaked out from her touching me.

But holy fucking hell, her mouth on me. I'm going to come, so fucking hard. Her head bobs up and down on my length, her tongue still licking my dick, all over like Ash Jnr is her favourite flavour of Paddle Pop.

And with a pop, she lifts her head up for a moment looking up at me with a sexy smirk.

"Fuck, temptress. You suck dick like a pro."

I'm throbbing so hard. I need to come. I give her a quick kiss, whispering against her lips, "Can I come in your mouth, temptress?"

She nods, taking Ash Jnr back between her pink lips, and I explode, shooting my load down her throat. And the damn temptress takes every last drop, looking up at me again as she swallows my load with a hard gulp.

Again I kiss her, pouring my thanks into the kiss.

"Thanks for that, temptress."

"You're welcome, Simba," she purrs at me, grabbing her bag from by her feet and getting out of the car.

Loathing Temptation

Tucking Ash Jnr back into my trackies I get out as well, slinging my bag over my shoulder. I grab Tem's hand, pulling her against me, my back against the car door. The first bell sounds, and I whisper in Tem's ear, "I'm returning the favour later, baby, but now get your sexy arse to class."

She sticks her tongue out at me, sauntering away. And damn she has a sexy arse, especially in a short skirt, with clearly only a g-string on underneath. I fucking love that my sexy temptress is coming out of her shell. But she's mine.

Yeah, I'm so whipped.

At Lunch, I'm sitting under the bleachers with Zeke. It's a nice day, cool but not cold and the sun is high.

I'm miles away though, thinking of this morning in my car, and thinking about tasting Tem's pussy again later. I'd been tempted to ask her to wag with me, to go home and play with—fuck—each other all day, but I knew she'd never go for skipping school. She might be a bit of a dirty girl underneath—and with me—but my temptress is still a good girl.

Breaking my dirty thoughts Zeke asks, with a mouthful of sandwich, "Ash man, you ok?"

"Yeah, fucking ripper," I reply, nodding and taking a final bite of my sandwich I didn't realise I'd even been eating, let alone polished off like a ravenous beast.

Zeke chuckles.

"You finally grew some balls and made her yours?"

I laugh, thinking back to Tempany asking me to *'fuck'* her. It's making Ash Jnr throb.

"She made me hers. Confessed she's in love with me," I tell my best mate, and his eyes boggle at me.

"Damn, man. That's sick."

"Yeah. And fuck I think I'm falling for her too. I shouldn't, but I can't help it."

"Yeah, that's sweet man. And I get ya," he tells me with a nod and a wink. "She's ya stepsister, but if your parents didn't get hitched then what would stop you being with her?"

Who is this 'oh wise guy' in front of me?

"Nothing man. I wanted her the moment I laid eyes on her again."

"Exactly," he practically sings. "And you're not falling, man. You're totally in love with her."

His words hit me hard. I honestly don't think I ever hated Tempany. I hated what she did, but never her.

"Yeah, I think I am," I tell my best mate, not able to hide my giddy grin. "But I'm not ready to tell her yet. I don't think our parents will like us being together."

"You never know," he replies with a shake of his head, and then a wink. He's acting odd. "But hey, sneaking around together is pretty damn tempting. Always turns me on when I got to sneak around for a root."

He did not. He did not just say what I think he did. He's totally fucked Ava. And I'm fuming.

"Tell me you didn't arsehole?" I stab at him.

"Didn't what?" he jeers with his cocky smirk.

Fuck I wanna slap him.

"You know what Ezekiel," I berate him. "Tell me you didn't fuck my little sister?"

Loathing Temptation

He laughs at me, clutching his stomach like what I've just said is the funniest thing on the planet.

"Oh shit man, Nah. I was talking about Lorena," he tells me once he's calmed down. "But yeah I've thought about fucking Av's."

That's it, I'm gonna kill him. *Fucking tosser.*

He continues, "Just not going to go there. I don't want my blood on your hands."

"Right, and yeah, touch her again and you're a dead man."

Again he laughs, and I wanna slap the smirk off his face.

"Noted," he tells me, his smirk disappearing when he continues, "And man, I'm sorry for being a dick to Tem."

"All good."

"It's just that riling her up is amusing, and we were out to ruin her before she took your balls so well you know."

"I said all good man but maybe you should grow some balls too, and apologise to her," I tell him. "She might not want to do the eisteddfod with your unapologetic arse."

"Yeah, I will. I'm not a complete tosser."

"Yeah, you are. But I love ya."

I take a swig of my chocolate milk smiling at him when he replies, "Back at ya, dufus. And speaking of music, I gotta get in early to hook up the equipment. Catch ya after school."

"No worries," I tell him as he stands up and walks off. I can't help but smile then thinking of Tem, and the fact that I don't hate her at all, not even a little bit.

Forty-Seven
Tempany

*G*etting to music class early to set up the equipment I'm taken aback when Zeke wanders in, early to. I'm still angry at him for the whole detention stunt. And he still walks around like he owns the place.

Ezekiel really rubs me the wrong way. I know he's Ashton's best friend, and Lorena's 'boyfriend', well 'sex friend' but I don't like him at all.

I scoff when he gives me a nod, thinking about walking out and going to the nurse to pretend to be sick, so I can go home and not have to spend the arvo pretending that I like Zeke. I'm at the

Loathing Temptation

door, but he stops me from crossing the threshold to leave, grabbing my arm and pulling me back into the room.

Yanking my arm back I screech at him angrily, "Don't touch me, Zeke."

He can't meet my eyes when he says, "Please Tem, can we talk for a minute?"

His tone seems sincere, so I reply, "Fine."

He sits down and nods to the seat across from him. I pull the chair out and sit down, telling him harshly, "Speak then. I'm listening."

He puts his head down for a moment, his elbows on his knees and mutters something I can't make out.

I poke his knee. "I can't hear you, dufus," I jeer at him.

He looks up smiling. And I'm worried his whole demeanour is all an act. Some other way to annoy me.

"I'm sorry Tempany," he starts, shocking me by actually using my full name. I didn't think he even knew it. "I shouldn't have said anything I did the other week."

He's got that right. I don't reply, so he continues in the same sincere tone, "I'm a dick. And I honestly didn't mean to get you upset."

"Well, you did," I tell him, with a soft smile. "I didn't expect that from you."

"Yeah, not my finest moments," he admits. "And I'm really hoping we can move past this, especially with the eisteddfod coming up..." His voice trails off. And I know I shouldn't but I throw him under the bus a little, to prolong his suffering.

"Yeah, I don't know. You really upset me, and I thought Ashton was your best friend. Does he know you came onto me?"

He laughs, his cocky smirk appearing on this face as he thinks for a moment before replying, "Yeah, he does. We don't keep secrets from each other."

"Oh um," I mutter biting down on my lip.

If Ashton knows about that, he's surely told his best friend that we had sex. I want the floor to break open and swallow me whole. Blushing I ask timidly, "Did he tell you anything about us?"

Zeke nods, still smirking and poking me in the ribs when he leans forward a little.

"Yeah, he told me he's in love with you," he informs me.

I playfully slap his arm.

"Yeah, right," I reply scoffing. "We might have slept together, but he doesn't love me."

Zeke doesn't bat an eyelid at my words, so clearly he knows about Ashton and me. But his reply shocks me.

"Believe me. My best mate is whipped for you, baby."

"Stop Zeke," I jeer, poking him again.

"Sorry," he says with a laugh. "So we good?"

I could be a bitch, but in this short conversation, I've seen a different side of Ezekiel. A side I don't think many people get to see.

"Yeah, we're good. Friends?"

"Definitely," he affirms as we stand up and he pulls me into a hug.

He squeezes me, before breaking the hug and looking at me with a sincere smile.

"I'm glad my best mate found his way back to you, Tempany," he tells me, happily.

Loathing Temptation

"Yeah, I..." I don't let the rest of the words out, not wanting to verbalise them to Zeke before I actually tell Ashton.

"You love him, I know. And he loves you too. Just give him time to get his head out of his arse to tell you."

"I will. Thanks for apologising. I know that wasn't easy."

"Damn right," he replies with a laugh, before elbowing in the side. "But honest, that's enough sappy shit. You ready to smash out our song?"

"So ready," I reply laughing.

The bell goes then, and we rush to quickly finish hooking up the equipment as our classmates' start to file in.

Zeke gives me a wink and grabs his guitar, slinging it over his shoulder to get ready to play.

Being in Lockgrove Bay is turning out to not be bad after all.

Forty-Eight

Ashton

Again Tem is wearing a sex kitten outfit, another short as shit skirt that practically shows her breakfast and this time a tank top, with a cardigan. And of course her knee-high socks. She'd only have to be wearing her hair in pigtails to be channelling Britney Spears in her *'Hit me baby, one more time'* days.

But no, my temptress has her long blonde hair loose, and it cascades down her back. The hallway is still full of people when I catch her at her locker at the start of lunch.

"Hey temptress," I murmur into her ear, stepping up behind her.

She turns to look at me, smiling.

"Hi Simba," she purrs, making Ash Jnr stir in my trackies. I groan, pushing her against the lockers.

"Damn temptress, I fucking love it when you call me Simba."

She taunts me, purring the nickname again, "Simba…" Her voice lingers on every syllable and I feel it everywhere, but especially in my daks. I'm so going to have a hard on in the middle of the corridor.

"Mmm Tem, you tease me," I tell her, licking my lips, and nodding to my semi in my daks. "And fuck I want you so bad right now."

"Oh really?" she teases.

"I've missed you, Temptress. Ash Jnr misses you."

"Stop, someone will hear you," she berates, but not able to hide the smile that curves the corner of her lips. I don't doubt my temptress is wet.

"Oh yeah?" I taunt kissing her neck, before whispering in her ear, "Follow me, Temptress."

I take her hand, not giving a flying fuck if anyone sees us and I drag her towards the library.

Considering it's lunchtime the library is surprisingly quiet. Tem is giggling as I drag her through the double doors, and straight toward the non-fiction shelving area at the back. No one is in sight. But still, the thought of getting caught is in my mind. And it's turning me on.

"Ashton, what are we doing back here?" Tem asks me curiously.

Shoving her against the bookshelves, I lean in, whispering in her ear seductively, "I'm going to fuck you, right here, right now against the shelves."

"We cant, Ashton," she says softly, almost protesting the advance. But she's smiling even when she continues, "Someone will see us or hear us."

Reaching down between our bodies, I run a finger along the seam of her pussy through her cotton knickers.

"So be it, temptress. But you can't deny just the thought of fucking in public is turning you on."

She doesn't reply, instead kisses me, taking my breath away. Her hands cup my cheeks, pulling me closer as the kiss deepens, and we're both panting for breath when we pull back a moment later. Ash Jnr is screaming in my daks, and with my forehead against Tem's I pull them down just enough to flip him out.

"Wrap your leg around my arse, baby," I whisper against Tem's lips. She follows the demand, her eyes not leaving mine, and reaching down between us I push the fabric of her knickers aside. And kissing her hard I slam my dick into her pussy. Against my lips she moans, lustfully, pushing her hips into mine.

Breaking the kiss, I grab her hands pushing them over her head, my eyes on hers and I thrust into her harder. She moans again, loudly, the force of our bodies slamming together knocking books to the floor.

"Oh my god, Ashton," Tempany screams out.

I'm not sure if it's in reaction to the books careening onto the floor, or my hard thrusts into her pussy. But I'm to lost in her to care.

Loathing Temptation

"I'm going to come," she tells me, letting out a moan when I still my thrusts.

"Me too, temptress. Kiss me," I demand, licking my lips with my eyes locked on hers. "Kiss me temptress, or I'll pull out before you get to come."

She cups my cheeks, pulling my lips to hers in a hot bruising kiss. And I thrust into her hard making her pussy throb around my dick, as she starts to climb to her peak. With one final thrust, whilst still kissing her I come, the same moment she crashes down with me, her whole body trembling.

Pulling out I quickly adjust myself, putting Ash Jnr back inside my daks. Tem bends down and starts gathering the books from the floor.

"Temptress, are you asking for round two?" I tease, playfully slapping her arse that's in the air, at exactly the right height when she bends over to pick up more books.

"No, but we need to pick these up," she says worriedly. "But that was hot and naughty. I'd do it again."

"Oh, I bet you would, temptress," I tease, taking her hand.

"We better head out before I'm tempted to skip class, and find somewhere else in this library to fuck you."

She giggles, kissing my cheek as we head out. The snotty dragon lady librarian at the front desk gives us dagger eyes as we walk out. And I give her an up yours, sticking my tongue out at her. She could do with some action.

She probably got off on hearing Tem and I together, because my temptress certainly wasn't quiet. I fucking love that. Fucking love that she's mine, and shows me with her moans and her kisses just how much she loves being with me. The feeling is most definitely mutual. I'd never have been so daring to fuck Fallon at school. I was never that horny around her that I had to have her at that very second. But with Tem around—my sexy temptress—Ash Jnr is pretty much semi hard every damn second. I think I'm in love with my stepsister. And it feels to good.

Zeke bails me up at my locker, clutching a basketball against his chest.

"Bro, I missed ya at lunch on the court," he tells me smirking. Shoving my books in, I grab my bag to sling over my shoulder.

"I was otherwise engaged."

"Oh right. Spill you horny bugger," he jeers at me, elbowing me as we start to head out of the building.

"I was in the library...with Tem."

"Seriously, man? You're that pussy whipped you're hanging out with her in the fucking library?" he asks, eyeing me questionably.

"We weren't just hanging out, dickwad," I tell him, with a wink. His eyes boggle, thoughts clearly in his dirty mind.

"Seriously, dude. You fucked her again? At school?"

"Yeah, man. Against the non-fiction shelves. And fuck I came hard."

"Ripper man. And damn, I didn't know Tem was a dirty girl." I knock the ball out of his grip.

"You have no idea," I reply laughing.

He snatches the ball back. "So you down for a game, dirty fucker?"

"Only if the girls can join."

Loathing Temptation

"Sweet. A little bit of two on two."

"Well, two on three. Kota is coming to hang today apparently."

Getting to the basketball court, I grab my phone out of my bag and throw my bag at the edge of the court. Zeke is already dribbling the ball, shooting for goal.

I quickly text Tem.

Temptress, b—ball game on the court now.

Ok but I'm keeping my clothes on

Of course temptress 😊

Putting my phone back in my bag, I head onto the court, stealing the ball off Zeke.

Barely a couple of minutes pass before the girls come running onto the court. Tempany winks at me, watching me as I dribble the ball across the court.

"You gonna steal my ball, temptress?" I taunt, smirking at her, and heading closer to her.

"Oh you bet I am, Ashton," she taunts. I let her steal it, stepping up behind her as she heads towards the goal to shoot.

She misses, and Zeke and I both laugh.

"Oh, Tem baby. You missed," Zeke teases, intercepting the ball and bouncing it back towards the other goal.

Ava steps into his face. Their eyes lock on each other, and he taunts her, "Av's you wanna touch my balls?"

I want to slap him for that comment. He still can't get the message through his thick skull that my little sister is off limits.

My little sister doesn't reply, instead, she slaps the ball right from his grip, and dribbles it away effortlessly whilst still glaring at my best mate.

"Oh damn Ava, baby," he taunts her again. "You're making me hard, Av's."

Oh no he fucking didn't! I'm on him, my fists balled. But don't get to lay a hand on him because Tem steps up behind me, wrapping her arms around me.

"Down, Simba," she whispers into my ear. I turn around in her arms, kissing her.

And again I want to slap my best mate when I hear his voice behind us, "Eww, Ash man. We don't need to see your pash sess."

I want to slap him so hard.

"You're being an arse, Ezekiel!" my sister yells at him, stepping closer to him and dribbling the ball in front of him.

She looks towards her best friend, and then back to Zeke who looks like he's thinking something really dirty. I don't even want to know.

"Oh, am I Av's? You telling me you're not wet for me?"

I want to scream and punch his fucking lights out.

Fuck! Let me at the fucker!

But I don't move, because I actually want to see how my fucktard of a best mate gets out of this himself without me intervening with my fists.

"No!" Ava bellows at him. "I don't want you, Ezekiel. Not when you're acting like an arsehole."

She reaches up to his cheek, the ball at their feet, bouncing low. And her hand slaps him hard across the cheek.

"Av's baby, that hurt," he says, wincing a little. "But I guess if you don't want me anymore, I could always get with Dakota," he taunts, giving Dakota a wink that makes her blush. Ava's best friend is really shy, and she's melting into a puddle just from Zeke looking at her.

I feel sorry for the girl. But still, I keep my trap shut because this shit show is fucking funny. I'm enjoying watching my little sister shoving my best mate under the bus.

"You will not!" Ava seethes. "Kota is too good for you, Ezekiel!" And with that taunt of his full name, she stomps on his foot and dashes over to me and Tem.

"Ashy I want to go home."

"Fine, Av's," I reply, looking at Dakota who is about to burst into tears. "Kota, are you still coming home with us?"

"Yeah," she mutters softly when Ava takes her hand.

The girls head off to my car, and I stare Zeke down for a moment.

"You're a fucking tosser, Zeke."

"At least I still have my balls."

"Yeah, go fuck yourself then," I yell at him, turning my back and grabbing my bag before running to my car.

My head is in a spin. I'm so angry at him for his words and so glad Ava put him in his place. But a part of me is upset, worried about him.

Shoving the thoughts aside when I get to the car I unlock the doors, and the girls all get in. Ava and Dakota in the back and Tem in the front with me.

As we drive off—to head home—Tem looks at me with a sweet smile, her hand on my thigh comfortingly. I need my temptress to help calm me down. And when we get home I know exactly how I'm going to do just that.

Getting home, the girls follow me inside. I'm dragging Tem up the stairs, with Ava glaring at me. At the landing, Tem kisses my cheek, dropping my hand and heading to the bathroom. Ash Jnr gets a kick out of that because I was thinking the exact same thoughts.

Our parents aren't home from work, so we're not likely to be interrupted. Ava pulls me aside before I can follow Tempany. "Kota, I'll meet you in my room. I just wanna talk to my brother for a minute," she says to her best friend who's rushing away towards Ava's room.

Dakota nods and Ava glares at me for a moment with her hands on her hips.

"So I'm guessing that something else happened with Te, Ashy?" she questions me.

"Might have. But none of your beeswax, Av's."

"Have you told her you love her?"

"I don't."

"Don't tell me porky's Ashy. You love her."

"Shut it Av's ok? And go be with Kota. I'm sorry about Zeke being an idiot."

"It's ok. I'll talk to Kota."

I nod and wait until she's headed into her room before I go into the bathroom.

Loathing Temptation

The water is already running, and the room is full of steam. Standing in front of the open shower cubicle I watch Tem for a moment. Her eyes are closed and she's tipping her head back under the water, lathering her hair with a shampoo that smells like roses. She's humming something. And I'm mesmerised by her, everything about her.

Watching her, I strip, stepping into the shower when she opens her eyes. My dick is aching, hard and ready to fuck her. Pulling her close I kiss her, my hand sliding between us to tease her whilst we kiss like we'll never get enough of each other.

I honestly doubt I could ever get enough of her. She reaches down to grab my dick, stroking it and biting down on my lip as she kisses me. I damn near explode from her naughty teasing. I break the kiss, grabbing her around the waist to turn her body around.

"Hands on the wall, temptress," I demand smirking at her.

She obeys, pushing her hands against the tiles, so her luscious arse is tempting me. Gripping her hips, I thrust inside her pussy. And she tips her head back to look at me, cursing out, "Oh fuck, Ashton!"

Still gripping her hips I start thrusting harder, slamming into her, loving the sound of our bodies smacking against each other.

Taking her hands off the wall, I'm still thrusting hard and deep inside her when she leans back against me, kissing me deeply, her tongue taking control of the hot kiss. God, it's fucking ecstasy.

I fucked Fallon in the shower a couple of times, and that was dismal, mediocre compared to this.

"Fuck Tem, fuck, baby," I scream out pulling out a moment and pushing her against the wall. I kiss her again, taking the control back this time and making her moan.

Lifting her leg up, I put it on my shoulder, sliding my dick back inside her and she moans so loudly I kiss her to silence her, thrusting harder and deeper to feel her moans against my lips.

Breaking the kiss panting she says raspy, "Ashton, fuck, fuck, I'm coming!"

"Me too, temptress. Come with me."

I thrust into her hard, feeling her start to spasm around me as I let go, filling her pussy with my load.

"Wow, Simba," she teases, giving me kiss after I put her leg back down and steady her against the wall. "That was hot."

"Oh yeah, Tem. Better get you clean now I got you all dirty," I tease, lathering her whole body up with soap.

She's smiling at me as we wash off the soap, and turn the water off before getting out and wrapping ourselves in fluffy white towels.

"Til later, Simba," she taunts, sauntering out of the bathroom after giving me a sexy wink.

My temptress has me in knots, and I think I've fallen for her.

Loathing Temptation

Forty-Nine

Ashton

With my hand on the doorknob of Miss Masters' office, I wonder if I should knock. I can hear her voice, but can't tell if she's on the phone or talking to someone.

Shrugging I push the door open, and my eyes fall out of my head in shock, and disgust. Miss Masters is bent over her desk and my dad is pounding into her from behind, his bare arse almost right in my face.

Screaming bloody murder, I slam the door and run, rubbing my eyes to try and get the horrible image out of my head.

Getting in the Camaro, I take in a deep breath starting the engine. My eyes are burning, I want to cut them out, but that wouldn't help. That image won't leave my head.

Caz May

Not only had I just seen my dad's ugly as fuck hairy arse but he was having sex with my principal.

Fuck!

I'm speeding home, thankful Tem isn't in the car with me today. We'd gone separately to school today, her car was running better and I had practice after school. I'm cursing myself for going to Miss Masters' office to ask about the scholarship. Because I will never get the image of that sight out of my head.

Taking the final corner towards home, I shake the thoughts away, stupidly closing my eyes for a second to blink back the hot tears stinging them.

Fuck, fuck! I curse, slamming my fist against the steering wheel. I don't know how it happens, but in that spilt second the Camaro careens over the curb and the engine is crushed against a tree, steam hissing out over the bonnet.

As if this arvo could be any fucking worse!

Yanking the door open, I stumble out, grabbing my bag from the passenger seat. It's only a block so I walk home, kicking stones on the road as I walk.

I'm so fucked. Dad is going to fucking kill me.

When I get home fifteen minutes later I grab an apple from the kitchen, and head upstairs to my room. Tem's door is open and I stop in her door jamb, leaning against it and taking a bite of my apple. She looks up at me from where she's sitting cross legged on her bed.

"Hey, Simba," she says softly, standing up and walking towards me.

"Hi Tem," I reply, taking another bite of my apple.

She stretches up to kiss my cheek.

"You ok?"

"No, I...fuck..." I curse dropping the apple on the floor, and wrapping her into a hug. Her arms wrap around me to, and I melt into her embrace. And the tears I was trying to hold in break free, starting to fall down my cheeks. Not wanting to be a pansy I sniff them away, and pull back from the hug.

"Ashton, seriously, what's wrong? Are you crying?"

"Yeah, nah...I...I crashed the Camaro."

"Oh no, how? Are you ok? Are you hurt?"

"I'm fine, not hurt...but...fuck..."

"What? Is something else wrong?" she asks, taking my hand and walking backwards towards her bed. She sits down and pulls me down with her, so we're lying side by side.

"Well, I...went to see Miss Masters after school about my scholarship."

"Yeah and what? Are you not getting it?"

"I don't know. I didn't get to speak to her."

"Oh why?"

I close my eyes, not able to look at Tem whilst I say the next words. "Because my dad was fucking her, bent over her desk."

I hear Tem gasp in shock, and she blurts out, "Oh my god Ashton! That's horrible."

Opening my eyes, I look straight into Tem's. She's just as shocked as I am.

"You have no idea."

"You need to report your dad to the school board, or something."

"I will, just not yet."

"Ok, are you going to be alright?"

"Yeah, Tem. But please, just kiss me."

She laughs softly, moving closer to me and pressing her lips to mine. I melt into the kiss, my heart hammering in my chest. And I get lost in kissing her, clearing my mind of everything but being with my temptress.

Twenty minutes later I'm still lying in bed with Tem, kissing her when my phone starts vibrating in my pocket. The staccato vibration isn't stopping, which means it's a phone call.

Breaking my kiss with Tem, I sit up on the edge of her bed, pulling out my phone and glaring at the flashing name on my screen.

Fidel.

I slide my finger across to accept his call, even though I'm petrified of hearing what he has to say. He doesn't even let me say anything though before he's bellowing, "I'm outside!"

I gulp, and reply as casually as I can muster, "Ok, but why?"

My heart rate is through the roof. Tem has sat up as well and she's sitting behind me, cautiously but there for me.

"I saw your car, Ashton Oliver," dad roars down the phone at me. "Get out here now boy!"

"Fuck you dad!" I scream at him, making Tem wince behind me.

"Don't you mouth off at me boy. You will get your arse down here now, or I'm beating the front door down."

"Fine!" I yell, throwing my phone on the floor furious.

I turn to look at Tem. She's shocked and heartbroken for me.

It fucking hurts.

Loathing Temptation

Frowning I get off the bed and press a kiss to her forehead.

"I'll be right back. Don't come outside."

"Ok, be careful Simba. I love you," she tells me, quickly giving me a soft, tender kiss before I walk out. I'm most likely walking outside to my doom. And I didn't tell Tem that I love her back.

I know I do love her, but letting those words fall from my lips is a lot harder than I ever thought it would be.

Storming out the front door moments later I confront dad, who's standing against his Maserati on the curb.

Caging him against the black metal I scream at him, "Go fuck yourself, dad!"

He stands taller, making me stumble a little but I don't move. "I crashed my car because I couldn't get the image of your bare arse fucking my principal out of my damn head," I seethe at him, shaking my head after I tell him the words and then locking my eyes back on his. They're dark, black like his fucking cold heart.

He shoves me back a little.

"You shouldn't be snooping. My personal life is not your concern."

"Seriously?" I bellow rhetorically. "You're fucking the principal of my damn school. And you don't even know how much of a hussy she is."

He balls his fists.

"What'd you say, boy?"

"She's a hussy," I tell him, trying not to smirk and let on that I'm about to tell a bit of a lie. "She came onto me, dad. She touched me in her office."

"You've some nerve boy," he berates me, his anger clearly starting to get the better of him. "Spitting out lies like that."

"It's true," I tell him, puffing my chest out. "And I'm going to bring you down daddy," I sneer.

He's seething and balls his fist again. I know what's coming, and I should move, run back into the house. But I know that running from my dad when he's enraged is asking for more punishment, and this time running away would be a death sentence. So I let him hit me, his punch crashing right into my jaw.

And motherfucking shitballs, it hurts. I can taste the blood in my mouth and stumbling back I don't even have a moment to think about fighting back or dodging his next hit because he's coming at me again, hitting my jaw on the other side even harder. The pain ricochets through my head.

And god I want to scream, but I keep the pain in check, wincing a little when I taunt him, "Good one dad. You gonna smack my arse too? Gonna tell me I'm a bad boy."

Dad is seething at me, just staring me down like he's processing my words and I look at his fists for a moment, which are covered in blood. Tentatively I touch my face, realising my nose is bleeding.

I turn away from him but he grabs me by the t-shirt, pulling me back and slamming my body into the side of the Maserati. Unbearable pain courses through my body. And I'm sure my body has made a dent in his black paintwork of his precious Maserati. The car he cares about more than his own flesh and blood. He can go fuck his ho in it for all I care.

"You child," he fumes in my ear holding my arms behind my back like I'm in handcuffs, "are a fucking cunt!"

Loathing Temptation

Craning my neck I turn to look at him, taking in a deep breath to hurl out an insult, "You teacher-fucking vile piece of oxygen stealing shit! You're a fucking arsehole 'dad'!" I bellow at him, right in his face so my spit hits his eyes.

He doesn't say a word, he's just fuming and turning red with anger. He yanks my hands above my head with one hand and pulls down my trackies with the other so my arse is bare.

Again I know exactly what is going to happen, and I'm powerless to stop it. I can't move, and I take in a breath, holding it in as I brace myself for the pain. And when I feel the smack of his palm across my arse I exhale the breath to stifle my scream.

"Smart move daddy," I taunt. "Beating my arse in the middle of the street."

He raises his hand again, and again I brace myself for the hit.

"Shut your fucking mouth child," he yells, slapping my arse harder, this time leaving an angry looking red mark against my lightly tanned skin.

He's still seething at me, and I'm bracing myself for another hit when he yanks my hands down from above my head and shoves me away like I'm nothing more than a piece of garbage. I fall to the ground, cursing under my breath when I land on my bruised arse. He stands over me, leaning over to beat his fist against my chest, winding me. I lift my arms up to try and fight back but he's too strong and the pain is making me breathless. And weak.

"You will keep your mouth shut, boy or I'll fucking shut you up for good," he threatens with a snarl. "You hear me?"

"Fuck you! I sneer, spitting at him and moving back on my hands before stumbling to my feet whilst he stalks off, getting in the Maserati (with the dent in the side) and speeding off without another word.

I pull up my trackies and go inside, wincing from the pain of my throbbing arse cheeks. The moment I step in the door, Tem is running down the stairs and wraps me into a hug. My whole body aches, but Tem's touch is healing and I melt into her hug, letting the tears fall. Pulling back from the hug, she takes my hand and helps me walk up the stairs to her bedroom.

She's crying too and I wipe the tears from her cheeks when we sit down on the bed together.

"Don't cry, baby. I'm ok."

"No, Ashton. You're not ok. You're bleeding, and clearly in a lot of pain. I...I..."

"Tem, I'm fine. Nothing some kisses from you can't fix."

"Um...ok. Let me get something to clean you up," she says with a slight smile, standing up and kissing my forehead.

The sweet caring gesture makes my heart beat hard in my chest. I'm in love with Tempany Davies. Never would I have thought that would happen when she sauntered back into Lockgrove Bay at the start of the year.

A couple of minutes later she comes back into the room with a face washer and a bottle of Dettol. Sitting back on the bed next to me, she wipes the warm face washer across my cheeks, and I wince from the pain, even though her touch is gentle.

"I'm sorry, Simba," she says sweetly.

"It's ok Tem. You're being gentle. It just hurts like a bitch."

"I bet. But you were so brave. Standing up to your dad like that."

Loathing Temptation

"Thanks, Tem. I don't feel brave. I couldn't even hit the fucker back."

"You were brave, and we're going to report him, so he can't do anything like this again."

"I know, Tem. I will do it, I promise."

"You better, or I will, Ashton. I love you, and I don't want to lose you."

I'm staring at her now, our eyes locked on each others.

My heart is hammering in my chest, and my brain is chanting the words, *'tell her, tell her you love her'*. But my tongue, well. "Tem, I...I..."

Tell her you idiot.

I try again, closing my eyes this time.

"Tempany, I lo..." But I don't get the words out, instead, she takes my breath and words away by kissing me.

And I know with this kiss that I'm hers forever, even if we can't be together a moment longer.

Fifty

Ashton

Sitting at the breakfast bar the next day after dad beat me I'm scooping cornflakes into my mouth, practically inhaling them because my head is so close to the bowl, so I can hide from mum's gaze under my baseball cap.

But mothers always know when something is wrong, and having a mum who is also a nurse—aged care—means things like cuts, bruises and black eyes don't stay hidden. She's always known in the past and was powerless to stop dad's beatings, but she doesn't know that he still beats me. And I intend to keep it that way.

Making a coffee, her eyes keep darting back to me. And I look up from under the cap, smiling at her to try and give her the sense

Loathing Temptation

I'm ok. The moment she notices the bruises on my face though, her face falls.

"Oh Ashton dear, how did you get those bruises? Is it from the accident?"

"Yeah, mum. I hit my face on the steering wheel when I crashed into the tree. I wasn't thinking straight, and I shouldn't have driven home."

She looks at me like I'm breaking her heart and takes a sip of her coffee.

"We should take you to hospital dear," she says calmly.

"I'm fine mum, really. Tem took care of me last night."

I'm sure she's going to tell me off for not going to the hospital, or calling the police about my accident, but instead, she nods, and says calmly again, "Oh yes. I noticed you weren't in your room last night when I came home. I missed saying goodnight."

I secretly love that she still likes to say goodnight when she comes home from work. I bite down on my lip, not able to meet her questioning gaze.

"Um, I was..." I mutter, cutting my words short. I can't admit to her that I was sleeping in Tempany's bed, kissing her and touching her until she moaned.

"In Te's room?" Mum asks her face lighting up with a smile that confuses me a little.

I'm wary when I reply, "Yeah I...I'm sorry mum."

I pull off my baseball cap and run a hand through my hair a moment. My stomach is in knots, wary of mum's caring tone, and smile.

"I know we can't really be together, but I...she...we..." I'm a blubbering mess of words. I honestly don't know what to say, not wanting to confess I'm in love with Tem to mum before I tell my girl herself.

I'd been so close to telling her last night, when we were in each other's arms and she was kissing and touching away the pain my dad inflicted on me.

Mum takes another sip of coffee, and I hastily gulp down a few mouthfuls of cornflakes, spitting the last bite back into the bowl when mum asks suddenly, "You love her don't you dear?"

Fuck what do I say to that question? Deny it? Confess.

Mum reaches out to touch my arm comfortingly, and the smile on her lips meets her eyes. She's not angry, and I feel relieved.

"Yeah mum I do but I can't really be with her and tell her how I feel because of you and Matias. He's your happy ever after, for real mum."

This time she smiles wider and laughs softly, sweetly.

"And Tempany is yours Ashton. If you really love her you have my blessing dear," she tells me warmly, squeezing my arm. "But maybe speak to her dad as well."

I smile back at her then, standing up and hugging her. I definitely won out in the mother department.

"Yeah, thanks mum. I love you and I'll speak to Matias."

"I'm sure he'll feel the same. Do you need a lift to school?"

"Nah, all good mum. Going with Tem. She'll be down in a minute."

"Ok, dear," she replies, kissing my forehead. "I'll see you tomorrow at brunch then. I'm working until midnight tonight."

"Pancakes and waffles Saturday family brunch?" I ask, grabbing a banana from the fruit bowl as I head out of the kitchen.

Loathing Temptation

"Sounds wonderful dear, if you're cooking?"

"Av's will," I call back with a laugh. "Have a good day mum."

"You too dear," I hear her voice call out, following me upstairs to Tem's room.

Reaching the landing, Tempany is coming out of her room with her bag slung over her shoulder. She looks absolutely gorgeous, beautiful actually, wearing floral velvet leggings and a black long-sleeved v neck t-shirt that shows a hint of cleavage. She steps closer to me, and I give her a quick kiss.

"You look sexy, temptress."

"You look sexy to Simba, but we can't."

I grab her around the waist.

"Yeah, we can, temptress. Mum knows about us."

"Oh my gosh, really? You told her?"

"No, she worked it out when I wasn't in my room again last night."

"Oh shit," Tem curses, biting down on her lip worriedly.

"Temptress, it's fine. Are you ready for school?"

"Yeah, are you sure you're up to going?"

"I'll lay low," I tell her, taking her hand as we head out to her car, where Ava is impatiently waiting for us.

I give Tem a wink as we get in her car, and Ava scoffs behind us in the backseat. I make a mental note to check in with my little sister when Tem turns up the radio, and we all start to sing along to 'Ashes'. Despite what happened with dad last night, and how much I'm worried about his threats I feel happier than I have since Tempany walked away with my basketball ten years ago.

Trudging into school, I pull my baseball cap down so it's over my eyes. Tem smiles at me from her locker, and heads to class. Zeke again bails me up, too eager for first period Maths class. The only good thing about today is it's Friday, and I have the whole weekend to spend with my family since we have a bye week, so no game or practice.

Zeke tips his head down to peer under my cap.

"Damn your car got you good," he jeers with a laugh. Sometimes I really hate him. When he says things before he actually thinks about what he's implying.

"Fuck off Ezekiel!" I sneer at him, about to grab my books out of my locker.

He looks at me with a sheepish smile.

"Oh sorry man. Didn't realise you were so pissy about losing ya wheels."

Grabbing him by the t-shirt I cage my best mate against the lockers.

"You know damn well these bruises are not from my fucking car."

He puts his hands against my chest, to calm me down.

"I'm sorry man. You need to bring the prick down, so he can't do this to you," he tells me with so much sincerity I'm shocked.

I let go of his t-shirt and he continues, "It's not right for a father to lay a hand on his son."

Stepping back I tell him, "I'm planning on it. Fidel Castello is going to burn in hell." *Where he belongs,* I add in my head, slamming my locker shut with my books now in hand.

Zeke laughs, slapping an arm against my back in jest.

Loathing Temptation

"Yeah, you gonna dig his grave? Can we throw him in it alive? Together?"

I can't help but laugh as well, at Zeke trying to lighten the moment.

"Nah, as much as I'd love to see the cunt suffer at my own hand, I'd rather avoid prison."

"Yeah man, I know. I'm sure you've got a plan."

He gives me a high five and we scoot into class when the bell goes.

Family brunch Saturday's are the best, chowing down on mountains of pancakes and waffles, covered in maple syrup and cream. It's been forever since we've had one, and today is extra special with Tem sitting next to me and Matias at the head of the table. I feel like an arsehole for ever thinking bad of him, about what happened in the past. I'm sure his side of the story is heartbreaking, just as much as Tempany's is.

Taking a final big bite of waffle, I swallow it down hard and look across to him at the head of the table. Nerves are bubbling in my stomach, and I'm regretting eating so much before having this conversation.

"Matias, could I...um...speak to you alone?"

"Sure, son, everything ok?"

My heart almost shatters from him calling me son, and not saying it with malice in his tone like my own father.

"Yeah, everything's fine," I reply as we both stand up from the dining table and he follows me into the lounge room.

He sits opposite me on the three-seater couch and smiles at me with genuine care.

"So, Ashton, what's going on?"

"I…um…I don't want you to hate me for what I'm going to tell you."

He looks at me again with his soft caring smile.

"I could never hate you, son. Is it ok if I call you son?"

I nod, replying, "Yes. But you might not want to call me that when I tell you how I feel."

He laughs but doesn't reply. Fuck, this so much harder than I thought it was going to be.

"Mr Davies, Matias, I'm in love with your daughter. And not as a stepsister."

"Oh, does Tempany feel the same?"

"Yeah, she's told me she loves me and we've…" I cut my words off. Confessing I took his daughters virginity probably isn't going to give me brownie points.

"I don't need to know details, but if you love my girl and she loves you back, then son, you have my blessing."

"Thank you, that means so much. I was so worried you'd think I wasn't good enough for Tem."

"You're more than good enough, Ashton. I hope we can build on our relationship, and get to know each other better."

"I'd like that, and thank you again."

"Anytime. I'm here for you whenever you need a man to man chat. And a game of basketball if needed."

"I'll probably whip you," I reply with a laugh, standing up from the couch.

He does the same and laughs, replying, "I don't doubt it."

Loathing Temptation

And before I can say anything else he pulls me into a hug, and my heart explodes with love. This feeling is amazing. And exactly what I've been missing my whole life.

The love of a father.

Fifty-One
Tempany

Making the phone call to the police about Ashton's dad was the hardest thing I'd ever done. Ashton hadn't made any attempt to do it himself, seeming to just have blocked it out like it didn't happen. I wasn't going to let that beating slide. The bruises still hadn't faded, even a week later and when we'd lay in bed together kissing he'd wince if I accidentally touched the bruises on his butt. It breaks my heart that he had to go through that and is still hurting so much from his father's heinous act.

I'd also contacted the school board, and Miss Masters was being dealt with for her dirty acts. Ashton didn't tell me, but I heard some rumours floating around school that she'd tried to hit on students, Ashton being one of them. That really pissed me off. And I know I shouldn't be doing what I'm about to, but I am.

I'm surprised I even remembered where Ashton's old house was, Castello castle as it was known around town. And I'm even more surprised driving up to the big cast-iron gates that they automatically open. Mr Castello probably doesn't even live here anymore, but I have to find out and confront him for what he did to his son, my Simba.

Pulling up in front of the house, and turning off the engine my nerves kick in. He's beaten his own son, and he'll probably not even care about his girlfriend coming to defend him. Taking a deep breath I get out of the car and walk up to the front door, scuffing my converse on the tiled portico.

The front door has one of those stupid lion knockers, and I laugh under my breath, thinking about my Simba as I grip it. Using the knocker I pound on the door a couple of times, taking a step back and shuffling on my feet nervously. Part of me is hoping that he doesn't still live here, and I can apologise and walk away with an 'I tried' mantra, but at the same time, I want to stand up to the arsehole.

The large door opens and my face falls, my heart hitting the ground. He—him—the man with the dark soulless eyes is standing in front of me, all dressed up in a black tuxedo. His dark eyes roam my body, hot lust flaring in them. I'm completely stupefied, but I can't move. He can't be Ashton's dad. This man cannot be my Simba's father. This man who tried to molest me after dad left because of mum's drinking. I'm taken aback, even more, when he opens his mouth to speak, "Well, well, if it isn't little Miss Tempany Davies."

He chuckles, almost manically, and my stomach lurches.

"Yes, and I'm here to tell you that I...I..." He cuts my words off, grabbing my arm and dragging me inside. Slamming the door behind me, he shoves me against it and steps closer to cage me in. He leans in, inhaling the smell of my hair.

"Tempany," he moans my name. "Still as alluring as ever. And now legal for me to have."

Taking a deep breath in, I let out a strong, "No! I will not let you fuck me or hurt me like you did to mum."

He steps back a little, raising his fist and my whole body tenses up. I still can't move away, and I know what's coming. But surely as cruel as he is, he wouldn't hit a girl.

"You say that like you have a choice, Tempany."

I gulp, cringing at the malice in his voice.

"You will let me fuck you, or I'll tell your daddy dearest what really happened to drive your mother to drink. "

"No!" I scream out, closing my eyes, bracing myself.

His fist moves up, and I feel the slap of his palm against my cheek. It's throbbing when I open my eyes and glare into them. "You're an arsehole! I know she lost your baby. And thank god, because you probably would've beaten him to."

"How dare you, Tempany!" he seethes, still glaring at me, and reaching down to touch me. My heart is hammering in my chest, but I'm not finished taunting the devil yet.

He grunts at me angrily, gripping my waist and pulling me towards his body.

Looking up at him, right into his cold eyes, I taunt viciously, "I've seen everything, Fidel. Everything you've inflicted on Ashton. And it's over."

Loathing Temptation

He seethes again, baring his teeth at me. And is about to kiss me when I stomp down on his foot, before pushing my knee up into his crotch. His arms fall from his grip on me, and he roars at me, "You fucking little bitch! A cocktease as always, just like your whore of a mother was. My cunt of a son can have you!"

He's clutching his crotch, hobbling towards me. And I swallow the lump in my throat, reaching down into my converse and pulling out the pocket knife. Flicking it open, I hold it out in front of me as a shield.

"You will not come closer to me or I'll hurt you." I stammer the words out, and Fidel laughs, manically again.

"You wouldn't dare child. What makes you think you can hurt me?"

He grabs me again, and with adrenaline coursing through my veins I fight back, pounding one fist against his chest, using the other hand to drag the knife down his torso from his neck to his groin. He lets out a bellowing horrific scream falling to the floor at my feet.

"Because I'm the one with the knife," I say heading out the door to my car.

I cannot believe I just did that. The adrenaline is still coursing through me and throwing the knife on the passenger seat I head home, ready to tell my Simba that I took his dad down.

Getting home, I grab the knife from the passenger seat, and rush inside, running straight up the stairs to Ashton's room. He's lying down on his bed, with a book in his hands.

"Simba, are you ok?" I ask.

"Yeah, ripper temptress, why?"

"You're reading a book," I reply laughing and practically skipping across to his bed.

"It's for English class," he tells me when I sit down next to him on the bed, putting the knife in my lap.

He eyes it with a smirk.

"You planning to kill me, temptress?"

"No, I ah...I went...to...see your dad."

He sits up, throwing his book aside.

"Why the fuck would you do that, Tempany?"

"To confront him, about what he did to you. To me."

Ashton seethes, his eyes locking on mine when he queries, "To you?"

I take in a deep breath, nervous to tell him about who his dad really is.

"He was the one who my mum was sleeping with before we left. He used to touch me."

"Oh fuck, Tem. You're shitting me yeah?"

"I wish I was Ashton. He's a horrible man."

"You've got that right baby," Ashton says softly, reaching up to cup my cheek and turn my gaze to his. I wince from the contact against my throbbing cheek.

"Ouch," I mutter under my breath.

"Did he hit you, Tem?"

"Yeah, but I fought back. I didn't let him touch me, and I kinda cut him and he fell to the floor."

Ashton laughs.

"You stabbed him?"

Loathing Temptation

"Well, not stabbed, but like sliced him. Still, I could've killed him," I say feeling panic suddenly hit me in the chest. I could've killed him. "Oh my god Ashton, seriously, what if I killed him?"

"Tempany, look at me," he says demandingly. I turn my head to lock on my eyes on his, my breathing panicky.

"You did not kill him. And if he dies because of this, because of what you, my brave girlfriend did, then it will be self defence."

"Really?" I mutter biting down on my lip, still anxious.

"Yes, baby. And to be honest, it would take a lot more to bring my fucker of a father down."

"True," I reply with a smile. "I also called the cops about what he did to you, and told the school board about Miss Masters too."

"Damn Temptress. You're fucking fierce, baby."

"You're not angry?"

"A little," he says. And I panic again. I don't want him to be mad at me.

"Oh, I'm sorry...I..."

"A little angry that you went to confront my dad without telling me, yes. But honestly Tem, I'm fucking proud of you, baby."

"Really?"

"Really, so throw that knife away and come here to kiss me. We'll deal with this shit later."

"I love you, Ashton," I tell him, throwing the knife from my lap to the floor and leaning over him, pushing his body down onto the bed to kiss him.

He doesn't reply with words, doesn't tell me he loves me back, but his kiss is so full of desire and 'love' I know my Simba feels the same as his temptress.

Fifty-Two

Ashton

After reporting my dad, Tem got a phone call to give more information. They wanted us to come in for some questioning, so I'm sitting next to Tem in an interview room at the cop station. I know I'm not a criminal but sitting in this room waiting for the cop is making me on edge. Tem puts a hand on my bouncing knee.

"You ok, Simba?" she asks softly.

"Nervous, temptress," I reply, kissing her forehead.

"Me too," she replies smiling at me when the cop walks in and sits down in the metal chair across from us.

"Great of you both to come in today. Don't be nervous. We just need to have some formal statements about the attacks from you mainly Ashton," the cop states, nodding at me. "And Tempany, we just need you to sign an affidavit that your actions were in self defence." Tem nods and the cop looks between us both.

"Great, so once these have been filed, what's the protocol for getting the fucker arrested?" I question, covering my mouth when I realise I just said *fucker* in front of a cop.

"Well, as we discussed with you both earlier, we have been and will continue to be on stakeout until he makes contact or attends the premises, at which time he will be arrested. These aren't the only charges against the accused."

"Awesome, thanks, Sergeant Booker."

"Not a problem, Ashton. So what else do you need to tell us about the incidents with the accused?"

Taking a deep breath, I relay the most recent beatings from my father, adding that he had been beating me since I was six. I also mention what happened with Miss Miller, and the exchange of money for the school in regard to that. Sergeant Booker nods on and off, writing down my words in scrawly handwriting.

When I finish he smiles.

"Great, that's all we need. We'll keep in contact, and please let us know if the accused makes contact with you also."

"Thank you," I reply standing up and taking Tem's hand with mine when she stands up to.

Sergeant Booker shakes our hands.

"Tempany if you could sign the affidavit at the desk on your way out that would be appreciated."

"No problems Sergeant."

He turns to walk out, looking at us both a moment.

"Look after each other. You make a sweet couple."

"Thanks, Sergeant, and we will," I reply, as he leaves the room with a nod. Heading out, Tempany signs the paperwork and we head home, on edge, but more than ready to bring my fucker of a father down for good.

It's been a couple of days after we met with Sergeant Booker, and the cops are still around the streets, patrolling and watching for the moment dad decides he's going to come and deal with us, like the threatened.

I'd been carrying my phone around with me, everywhere, with a portable battery charger attached so it never went flat, just in case I need to dial triple zero in a hurry.

The whole thing, even though the police are equipped to handle it has me on edge. I'm standing in Tem's room, gazing out her window, anxiously looking around for a black Maserati with a dint in the side.

For all I know, the fucker probably fixed it, but I can only hope he didn't and that either myself or the cops will recognise the car. Tem is hugging me from behind, trying to soothe me and calm me down.

"Simba, it will be ok. You know he won't be able to resist coming back."

I'm about to reply when I see a black Maserati turning into the street. My finger slams into my phone, dialling triple zero, but it's not necessary. The cops saw to, and they're moving in on dad's pride and joy. One cop car stops in front, another behind when he pulls up on the curb. My stomach lurches, thinking about what he did to me that day in the exact same spot.

Loathing Temptation

The fucker slides out, smoothing down his suit and eyeing the cops, giving them a curt nod. I wanna run outside and throw something at his head, to scream and yell at him. To tell him that I absolutely fucking hate him and that he should burn in hell for eternity.

Of course, I don't do that. I grip the window sill, not able to tear my eyes away from the scene below. I tense up in Tem's arms, and she says softly, "You think we should go out there?"

I turn in her arms, kissing her softly.

"Only if you come with me. I do kinda wanna watch from closer."

We run down the stairs, our fingers laced together. Pushing open the front door, we stand on the porch, and I pull Tem to my side with my other hand. I kiss the side of her head and turn my attention to the scene in front of me.

Running downstairs we missed a bit, but the cops have dad up against the cop car with his hands behind his back. He's screeching at them, "Get your hands off me fuckers."

"No can do. You're under arrest for non-aggravated assault, sexual assault of a minor and other related charges that will be detailed to you in court proceedings. You do not have to say or do anything, but if you do, it may be used in evidence against you."

Dad spits on the ground, and the officer locks his hands into the cuffs, pulling him back and shoving him inside the open door of the cop car.

He gives me an up yours gesture, screaming out, "Fuck you, bastard son. You'll curse this day Ashton Oliver Castello!"

The officer slams the car door, giving Tem and I a nod. Another officer comes over to us, smiling, which makes me feel kinda giddy too.

"Thank you both for your assistance in this arrest. We'll let you know if we need anything else and the court date details. Have a good night now."

The cop cars leave, and a tow truck pulls up, making quick work of securing dad's Maserati to the back. For a moment I want to tell him to leave it, so I can drive it and smash it, but Tem squeezes my hand and smiles at me.

"Well, that was crazy," she says with a laugh.

"Yeah, definitely. Let's head inside."

She follows me in, and up the stairs again. A whirlwind of emotions are making my head spin, and now there is only one thing I want to do, glad we have the house to ourselves for a few more hours.

Tem is sitting on my bed, her legs crossed and she's looking at me smiling. The sweet smile that makes my insides feel alive. We're both still mind blown by what happened with dad and I want to forget it and enjoy Tem's company, but I know that firstly I need to use some words.

"Tem, baby, I need to say something."

Her eyes light up, and she moves to lay down next to me, running her fingers across my arm. The sweet touch gives me goosebumps.

"Yeah, what's that?"

I turn onto my side to look at her, kissing her forehead.

Loathing Temptation

"I'm sorry Tempany, for everything. For taunting you, and all the mean as fuck words I hurled at you. I'm sorry for what my dad did to you, and all the pain you had to endure because of that."

"Oh, Ashton, thanks. I appreciate that so much," she says giving me a quick, sweet kiss. "I'm sorry for taking your basketball all those years ago."

"The past Tem," I remind her. "And I only want to think of the future with you. The future with you as my girlfriend."

She lets out a little girlish squeal.

"You really want me to be your girlfriend?"

"Yeah, temptress I do. Because..." I pause, taking in a deep breath, and leaning closer so I'm almost kissing her.

"Because?" she asks, the question a vibration against my lips that sends a jolt through my whole body.

"Because I love you Tempany. I'm absolutely, completely and wholeheartedly in love with you."

She murmurs, pressing her body closer to mine, kissing me, taking my breath away. Against my lips pulling back but still close, she whispers, "I love you Ashton, my Simba."

I feel those words through my entire body. Tempany has my whole heart, and breaking the kiss I gaze at her for a moment before smirking at her when I put a hand up underneath her t-shirt.

"Tem, I want to make love to you."

A sweet giddy smile lights up her face, and she doesn't say anything, instead, she sits up, lifting her t-shirt over her head, and unclasping her bra so it falls down her arms. Her body is exquisite and all mine.

Caz May

"Mmm, fuck temptress you're perfection," I murmur taking one of her nipples into my mouth. She moans, arching her back, writhing from the touch, the lick of my tongue over her sensitive buds. Turning my attention to the other one, I slide my hand into her leggings, to find her pussy bare.

"Commando, temptress, you're a dirty girl."

She laughs, cupping my cheeks and pulling my face to hers for a hungry kiss.

"Only for you, Simba."

Breaking the kiss, I trail kisses down over her tits again, across her stomach until I reach her leggings. Yanking them down I flick my finger over her clit, making a moan escape her lips before she purrs, "Taste me please, Simba." The way the nickname rolls off her tongue, a literal purr of the word makes my dick throb in my daks. I want to sink inside her, make love to her, and then fuck her until she's screaming my name, but first I need to make her come with my tongue. Pleasure for my temptress, the only girl I've ever loved.

Kissing the inside of her thighs, I yank her leggings to the floor. And without giving her any warning I kiss her bare pussy, slipping my tongue inside her and sucking on her sensitive bud.

"Oh fuck, Ashton, more please...more," she calls out between moans that are making me throb so much I know I'm already leaking pre-cum. I keep licking, swirling my tongue in and out and nudging her clit with my teeth. Her hips buck up to my face, urging me on. I can tell she's close. Her pussy is starting to pulse beneath my tongue.

Loathing Temptation

"Fuck, Ashton, I'm coming," she calls out gripping the sheets in her fists, writhing on them and moaning loudly as she comes all over my face.

Sitting up again, I lick my lips, smirking at her, "Mmm, temptress, you taste delicious baby."

She laughs as well, grabbing my t-shirt to pull me down for a kiss. She licks my lips, tasting herself on them, and lets out a moan that nearly makes me embarrass myself.

Breaking the kiss, before I can even think she's yanking my t-shirt off, her fingers trailing down my abs to my v muscles. She pulls at the waistband of my trackies, teasing me, "Are you commando too, Simba?"

"Find out temptress," I tease back, her hand sliding inside my trackies to grip my dick. *And oh holy fuck!* Nothing—other than being inside her—feels better than her soft hands on me. Nothing will ever feel like her touch.

"Mmm, you're a dirty boy, Ashton," she taunts, dakking me without warning. I lie over her, kicking my trackies off at from my ankles. And I kiss her, my dick slipping inside her and making us one again. I lay still for a moment, still kissing her whilst seated inside her pussy.

Just being inside her, without moving makes me feel complete, as though I've been waiting my whole life for her. Breaking the kiss, I slowly start to thrust in and out. Her legs wrap around my arse, pulling me in deep to fill her completely. She's panting and letting out sweet moans. And with a final thrust, I feel her pussy clenching, her body trembling as we let go together.

"I love you Tempany," I call out, kissing her as I tremble from the aftershocks of my climax.

"I love you to, Ashton. I always have."

Pulling out I lay beside her, and she snuggles against me.

"I think I loved you since you first played basketball with me."

"Yeah, me too," she replies, kissing me breathless again.

There's nowhere else I'd rather be.

Fifty-Three

Tempany

T he last couple of months had been hectic, full of some things amazing, and some things that were horrible and heartbreaking. Ashton's dad's court date was looming, and even though Ashton had tried to at least be forgiving his dad completely shut him out, refusing to even see him.

It broke my heart, but Ashton shrugged it off to focus on his last months of school and exams. We enjoyed being together, most nights sleeping in the same bed, sometimes his room and sometimes mine. But neither of us mentioned what was going to happen next year when the boys were going to leave for Uni.

Caz May

There'd just been too much going on, and we were in the new love bubble.

Today though, I'm nervous about the eisteddfod. I've put on my most formal outfit, a knee-length pencil skirt and white long-sleeved blouse with a ruffle at the front. Ashton comes up behind me whilst I'm applying some makeup in the bathroom mirror. He kisses my neck, his eyes locking on mine in the mirror.

"You look beautiful, Tem. You and Zeke are gonna knock the judges dead with your song." I turn in his embrace, kissing him.

"I hope so, Ash. I'm so nervous."

"You'll be amazing. You ready to head out? We need to pick Zeke up on the way."

"Yeah, I'm ready," I reply, taking his hand with mine to head out of the bathroom.

After picking Zeke up, we get to the auditorium in record time. The nerves are still bubbling in my stomach, and getting out of the car Zeke grabs his guitar out of the boot, whilst Ashton pushes me up against the car kissing me, hard and hungrily.

"Still nervous, temptress?" he asks.

"A little," I tell him, kissing him again.

Zeke scoffs, leaning against the car next to me.

"Seriously, we're outside," he sneers.

Ashton breaks the kiss.

"Rein in ya jealousy, tosser."

"Will do when you keep the PDA away from my eyes."

"I'm just trying to calm my girlfriend down, but you don't know the meaning of the word girlfriend."

Loathing Temptation

Zeke rolls his eyes and starts walking inside, with Ashton and I following holding hands. His presence is definitely making me feel calmer.

Once inside, he heads to his seat after giving me a soft sweet kiss. I head backstage and find Zeke tuning his guitar, strumming it whilst he stands against the wall in the wings waiting to go on stage. We're one of the first to perform which I'm happy about. Standing next to him he elbows me in the side.

"Sorry about before. I shouldn't be jealous of you and Ash."

"It's ok. I get it. But can I ask you something?"

"Yeah, sure, I guess."

"What happened with you and Lorena?"

He laughs under his breath.

"We fucked a couple of times. And she wanted to be my girlfriend, but I can't do the whole girlfriend thing."

"Yeah, why? Lo really liked you."

"I...I'm in love with someone else," he tells me. I'm not able to reply, as the first performers start on stage and we're silenced by someone with a headset walking thorough the wings.

The first performance is a dance trope and they're good, really good. It makes the nerves bubble in my stomach again. Zeke gives me a smile as they rush off stage, and we head on. He pulls two stools onto the stage, and I sit on one whilst he plugs his guitar into the amp next to the other stool.

The spotlights focus on us, and he starts strumming out the melody of the song. Patting my hand against my thigh softly, I count the beat ready for my intro. And when it's time I close my eyes, open my mouth and let out the words, 'Oh, oh, I'm on a high, oh oh, I'm tempted by you.'

I sing out the rest of the words, losing myself in the melody and words Zeke created. My heart is hammering in my chest, and as I sing the last words, 'I'm free falling, in love with you,' I wonder who the song is really about, who Zeke is in love with that doesn't love him back.

We head off the stage, down to the dressing rooms and wait for the rest of the performances. I make small talk with Zeke to pass the time.

"Are you looking forward to next year? I ask him, smiling.

"Yeah, I've always wanted to go to the institute of music. Dream come true."

"I'm really happy for you, and for Ashton getting into Deakin to." I frown, thinking about my boyfriend leaving me behind to go to university. We still have a couple of months together, so I need to focus on the time we have left together.

"Thanks, and yeah it's pretty sick. But I…"

"You're going to miss her? Who the song is about?" I question him.

He looks at the floor, then up at me, muttering, "It's Ava."

I gape at his words, and then smile at him.

"You're in love with Ava?"

"Yeah, and seriously don't tell Ash. It's a good thing we're leaving because at least I'll be away from her and can move on."

"I'm sorry Zeke. Our secret, I promise," I tell him, giving him a hug.

After all the performances are done, the winners are announced not long after. Zeke and I win 'Best original song' and

304   *Loathing Temptation*

'Best duet performance'. Walking back off the stage holding the awards, I'm giddy and rush out to meet Ashton.

Zeke and I both shocked that both of our parents and our siblings are waiting for us in the foyer. They hug us, congratulating us.

"So it seems a celebratory dinner at Enzo's is in order," my dad says, glancing around at everyone.

"Sounds wonderful," Mrs Alessio replies. "We will meet you there." She kisses Zeke on the forehead. "I'm so proud of you, son."

"Thanks mum, we'll see you at Enzo's."

We all head out to our cars to go and celebrate. And taking Ashton's hand as we walk out I can't help but smile. I'm so happy he's mine, and so happy I came back to Lockgrove Bay.

The last few weeks of school flew by way to quickly. All I can think about—even now when I'm sitting with our families in the school auditorium on fold out chairs—is that it's only a couple more months until the boys leave; until Ashton leaves.

I need to shake those thoughts away to focus on the boys' graduation. I look up to the stage, hearing them announce Zeke's name first. He saunters up onto the stage, taking his diploma and shaking Miss Masters' hand. I'm surprised they let her finish the school year as principal, but considering there was no evidence that anything happened with students and her misconduct was only with a parent she was still allowed to be at graduation.

Zeke hollers , "Hell yeah, I graduated!' as he walks off the stage, back to his seat. A few more names are called before they get to Ashton, and he rushes up on the stage, refusing to shake Miss Masters' hand. He grabs his diploma, turns around and lifts up his graduation gown to moon the audience.

"Hell yeah, I graduated!" he hollers, and then turns to Miss Masters. "And you can kiss my arse!"

He runs off the stage, blowing a kiss to me as he heads back to his seat.

The rest of the ceremony is pretty uneventful, the graduating class excepting their diploma's before all heading up onto the stage again for a photo and the throwing of their caps.

Afterwards, people are gathered outside hugging and congratulating each other. Ashton rushes up to me, kissing me. "Congrats, Simba," I taunt him, grabbing his butt through the gown he's still wearing. "Trust you to be commando under your gown."

"You love it, temptress. Are you ready for a ripper night of celebrating? Now it's also your night of turning legal?"

"Definitely," I reply, laughing. He gets a hug from his parents and Ava, giving her a nod. She nods back, pulling something out of her handbag. Ashton smiles at me, after taking a small velvet box from Ava.

When taking my hands, for a moment I think he's about to drop to his knees, to pop the question, but he doesn't. He opens the box, holding it up to me.

Inside is a heart locket, with 'A & T 4eva' engraved on it.

Ashton kisses me, and says, "Happy eighteenth birthday, Tempany. I love you."

"Oh Ashton, I love it and you."

Loathing Temptation

He takes it out of the box and I turn around so he can put it on me. He gives me another sweet kiss, and our parents and Ava collectively sigh.

"Time to celebrate these two events in your lives," Sascha says. "We're so proud of you both, and we love you both."

She pulls me into a hug, before all head to the car to go and celebrate.

I know this is true happiness, and what Ashton and I share is true love. Falling in love with him has been so amazing, and having him love me back makes me feel like a queen.

I fell in love when I was six years old, with my very own Simba, my protector and forever love, Ashton Oliver Castello.

He may have loathed me, and been tempted by me when he shouldn't have been, but now I know that he fell in love with me to, all those years ago.

And no matter what happens now, I have no regrets crossing the line from hate to love.

Epilogue

Ashton

I t's crazy how much can change in a year. How your life can go from being a shit show to amazing in twelve months.

A year ago, days after I'd celebrated my eighteenth birthday Fallon dropped her bombshell on me, her fake pregnancy and I'd broken up with her, my girlfriend of two years.

But now standing on the beach—in front of a huge bonfire, even though it's a warm January evening—I'm surrounded by my friends to celebrate Australia day and my Nineteenth birthday and I'm watching my new girlfriend walking towards me.

My Tempany looks stunning, wearing the same black triangle bikini she was wearing last year when we came to the beach with

Loathing Temptation

Ava to get to know each other. I'd wanted to get to know her with a kiss, and all sorts of dirty ways.

And we'd done that and then some. She was a temptress for sure.

Sashaying her hips, she comes towards me, handing me a beer. "Happy birthday, Simba," she says clinking her Vodka cruiser bottle against my beer bottle. We both raise them to our lips to take a sip of our drinks.

"Thanks, temptress," I reply giving her a kiss.

We sit down on the sand next to the bonfire, drinking and holding hands, enjoying being together. Someone hollers from the shoreline to turn the music up, and I see Zeke running over to my Mustang, and turning the volume knob so the music shakes the whole car.

After crashing the Camaro last year, after the shit storm that happened with my dad I'd gotten my trust fund earlier and bought a brand new red convertible mustang with black stripes over the bonnet. It certainly turned a few eyes when I drove it around town with the top down, and Tem sitting next to me.

With the music pumping, and people drinking the party was really starting to heat up. A couple of my old teammates were cooking sausages in the bonfire, to wrap in bread in true Australia day celebration sausage sizzle style.

I look at Tem, asking, "Do you want a sausage?"

Her eyes gaze over my body when I stand up. I'm only wearing board shorts, and her appreciative gaze makes my dick jolt in them.

"Not my sausage, temptress," I jeer at her with a smirk and a wink. She laughs.

"Oh, no thanks, I'm fine," she replies, taking another sip of her drink.

"Ok, baby, I'm going to go grab one. I'll be back in a minute."

Heading over to the guys I'm sidelined by Beau.

"Hey man, happy birthday."

"Thanks, man. How's things?"

"Not bad, man. Just wanted to catch ya and apologise for the shit with Fallon."

I eye him. He's nervous, looking down at the sand with his hands in the pockets of his denim shorts.

"All good, man. It's in the past."

"Yeah, I'm happy you found Tempany. She's a great girl."

"Yeah, she is. I'm going to miss her so much this year."

"Yeah, sucks. But yeah I'm honestly sorry about the whole cheating fiasco with Fallon."

"I know Beau. It's cool man. Have you spoken to her?"

"Yeah, only to find out as you probably knew that the kid was mine. But last I heard she miscarried. And she shut me out."

"Oh shit man, I'm sorry. That sucks."

"Yeah, I fucking loved her. But yeah, wasn't meant to be."

"Yeah, anyway man. Thanks for coming. I'm going to go grab a snag and head back to my girl."

"Sweet man, enjoy the rest of ya night. Might catch ya in the city sometime." He walks off, and Zeke comes up to me slapping me on the back.

"What'd Beau want?" he asks, taking a sip of the beer in his hand.

"Just apologised for cheating with Fallon, and told me she miscarried."

"Oh shit, that's horrible. But bullet dodged with Fallon for sure."

"Yeah, she was never the right girl for me."

"Yeah, Tem's definitely your endgame."

He looks at me with a hint of sadness in his eyes, again taking a gulp of his beer to try and hide his emotions from me. My best mate wears his heart on his sleeve though, and can never hide how he feels.

"You'll find your girl Zeke."

"Yeah," he mutters, not meeting my eyes on his. He wants to say something else, but I don't probe him. "Enough sappy shit, bro. Grab a snag with me, and then we can get this party really started."

We both grab sausages, and another beer each before I go back to sit with Tem.

After a few hours, people have started heading off, the drinks have dwindled down to nothing and the bonfire is slowing to a low simmering flame.

Zeke comes over to Tem and I giving me a side hug.

"Catch ya, bro. Hope you had a grouse birthday."

"Thanks man," I reply as he heads off.

I take Tem's hand then, pulling her up off the sand. I kiss her hard, and smile against her lips.

"I love you Tem," I tell her, taking her hand in mine.

"I love you to Ashton," she replies, kissing me again.

Breaking the kiss, I drag her down the beach, dropping her hand at the water's edge. I yank my board shorts down, smirking at her.

"You up for skinny dipping with me temptress?" I tease.

"Oh you bet I am Simba," she teases back, undoing the ties of her bikini top and pushing the bottoms to her feet to kick them off.

When she's naked I grab her around the waist, throwing her over my shoulder and running into the surf.

Putting her down in the water, I pull her body against mine, wrapping my arms around her before kissing her again, a deep sweet kiss to tell her that no matter where I am, she's my forever. My temptress, my queen, and I'm her Simba, her king.

Loathing Temptation

Australian Slang Glossary

Ute-Truck

Bludger- someone lazy, doesn't do much and possibly relies on social security benefits

Ripper- something really good/great

Ridgy-Didge- Cool

Bonzer-Great, awesome

Pash/ing/ed- to kiss/make out

Arvo- afternoon

Chunder- Vomit, throw up

Gobby- Blowjob

Aussie Kiss- going down on a girl

Daks- pants/trousers/underwear

Undies/Knickers/Jocks-underwear (female knickers, male Jocks, undies both)

Dakking/ed- to pull or have pulled someone daks down (see above)

Bathers- universal name for female swimwear

Budgie Smugglers- small male swimmer that looks like underwear (google this one to see)

Thongs- Footwear, otherwise known as flip flops

Esky- Cooler-you keep drinks cool in it

Dunny- toilet

Bogan-white trash/trailer trash

Old Fella- Your father/Dad

Franger- Condom, Trojan etc

Milo- a malt chocolate powered drink mix (can be made hot or cold)

Caz May

Macca's-MacDonalds

Fair Dinkum- used to emphasise or seek confirmation of the genuineness or truth of something

Fucking/Bloody oath- similar to above, but an extreme or emphasised way of saying yes.

Shark Week/Rags- A woman's monthly cycle

Stuffed if I know- a nicer way to say fucked if I know

AFL- Australian Rules Football

Fuck me dead.-oh my god, holy hell, struck dumb

Grouse- Describe something as great, terrific or good.

Giving me a view of her breakfast- showing your underwear from clothes to short.

Stalk Me

Instagram- @cazmayauthor

Facebook- @CazMayAuthor

BookBub-Caz May https://www.bookbub.com/profile/caz-may

Spotify- cazcat25

Goodreads https://www.goodreads.com/cazmay

Acknowledgments

Hey lovely readers!

This time I need to shoutout to some special people who have made writing this book a pleasure.

Samantha Wolf (@wolfluna101 Instagram) Girl, as an early reader of this book as I wrote it, your support means the world. Thank you for letting me bounce ideas off you, crazy ones and everything in between. Writing this book wouldn't have been so wonderful without you.

Elysha (@booktiqu.e Instagram) My fellow crazy Aussie! I love you, and your reaction to my boys. Your support and love of this book from the moment I shared it with you as a beta reader spurred me on to keep writing it. Your support has meant the absolute world, and I'm glad we found each other.

As always, **my bestie, Bianca.** I love you, B. I think a bit of my cheeky sassy Lorena is you. Thank you for your unwavering support and love. I miss you so much and being able to share my books with you means so much. No matter what I'll always write for you.

And my bearded hero, **my husband Cam.** He puts up with me, when all I'm doing is writing and love will never be enough to describe how much he means to me.

If you've enjoyed this story, then please review on Amazon and any other platforms you can.

And also I thank all of you who've taken the time to read this book, and any of my other books. Your support means the world! I love you all and appreciate each and every one of you! Signing off! For now! Until the next book!

Caz May xx

Loathing Temptation

Caz May

CPSIA information can be obtained
at www.ICGtesting.com
Printed in the USA
LVHW010545281220
675196LV00005B/100